The
Forgotten

By

Spencer Hawke

Spencer Hawke

ISBN-10: 1515375633
ISBN-13: 978-1515375630

DEDICATION

An Author finds inspiration in many unusual places. My lucky break came when I met my wife Jenny some 25 years ago. I didn't know it then, but I was marrying an Angel. Rarely does one meet such a wonderful woman. What makes her so unusual is that not only is she a beauty to look at, but her goodliness and Godliness are even more incredible. I am a lucky man indeed. In fact, if she had not introduced me to her family in Altus, Oklahoma these pages would not have been written.

Not many people outside of the State of Oklahoma have been to or know of Altus. It sits on the South West Plains of the State and produces many fine crops of cotton, corn and great American families.

I met one such family many years ago, at the time the patriarchs of the family was a God fearing, soon to be centenarian, his son in law, who never met an old car he didn't love (or buy for his collection) and his son in law who, as the youngest of the trio was constantly kept busy protecting the extended family, and on the side managing to find time to run a very successful business.

This family were all home to attend the annual Thanksgiving Celebration. On this occasion, son K, who has a passion for fast cars. was off tearing up dirt roads in one of his souped upped hot roads, leaving me time to attend a family lunch and catch up on family news.

It was on this occasion that I first learned about Kalamata, Greece. Daughter K, who besides being much more scholastically inclined than her brother, was in the process of deciding whether to dedicate her life to those less fortunate than herself.

It was at this luncheon that I first learned about daughter K's odyssey through the roads less travelled of Europe, dedicating her time to help some of the victims of Europe's sex trafficking trade. Mom K beamed with pride as she told me about her daughter's commitment and then turned very serious as she recounted the terrible travesty this so called modern society allows to be perpetrated against our youth.

While pompous politicians belch over their taxpayer funded extravagant lunches, real Americans are trying to do something about the horrors many precious fallible children of God are destined to suffer through.

Hopefully this book will help inspire at least one leader to skip a lunch and DO SOMETHING. If not the Greek Goddess Artemis, the daughter of Zeus and Leto, the protector of young girls and boys, might decide to bring her fury to bear on those that ignore this horrific problem.

This work, is my attempt to spread the word with many thanks to those special people in Altus.

If you wonder why this book is more expensive than the first two books in the Ari Cohen series, it is because a portion of these proceeds go to fund organizations that I feel are trying to fight this injustice. If you and your business would like to buy bulk personalized quantities of The Forgotten to make your business customers aware of this injustice email me spencer@spencerhawke.com

PROLOGUE

PERIL ON THE HIGH SEAS: MEDITERRANEAN 75 BC

The slavers came after the Herculaneum soon after she set sail on the high tide. She had recently docked in the ancient Roman port of Ostia, after a voyage across the Aegean Sea. Her cargo had been honey and olives, taken on board in Pergamon in modern day Turkey. The honey was used extensively as a sweetener, but also to make mead, better known as honey wine.

Her journey had been uneventful. The Herculaneum had crossed the Aegean Sea, sailing westwards until landfall was spotted. Then she changed course heading due south, relieved to be within sight of land. She had followed the boot leg of Southern Italy, in the relatively safe waters patrolled by the Roman Navy.

Outside the coastal waters of the Roman Empire, pirates dominated the Mediterranean. Travel by sea, away from the territorial waters was only undertaken when absolutely necessary.

The Roman Empire, at that time, was the only major Mediterranean power. Her Navy, primarily Merchant Marine, was designed to supply land based outposts and colonies.

Rome only protected the sea lanes on either coast stretching from Corsica and Sardinia on the west coast and Greece and Albania on the east. The rest of the Mediterranean was the refuge of buccaneers and cut-throats.

Smaller communities in Greece, Turkey and North Africa were left to make their own security arrangements with these brigands. Those unable to fend off the pirate incursions were forced to come to an understanding with the raiders or suffer the consequences. Most communities capitulated, thus becoming safe havens.

As soon as the Herculaneum had emptied her cargo she was made ready for her next voyage. Spies in port were the first to notice the unusual cargo being loaded on board. Trunks of finery, preserved food, the finest of wines... as if a noblemen and his entourage were going to board.....

Word soon spread, eyes were watching; perhaps there was money to be made.

The main trade of the pirates, even in those days was slavery. Roman merchants bought slaves for their ever-growing plantations and the Roman Navy needed oarsmen.

The Islands of Delos and Rhodes in Greece became the center of the Mediterranean slave market. At its heyday, 100,000 slaves passed through its markets in a single day.

The Herculaneum had been made ready, her important passenger Gaius Augustus, soon boarded. Before long word spread that he was going to study philosophy and public speaking in Rhodes.

What was of more interest to the pirate's spies was the destination. The route the Herculaneum would have to take to reach Rhodes would mean sailing more than 250 miles south along the Roman Navy patrolled coast, before rounding Sicily. Then she would have to traverse 500 miles of lonely, open sea, unprotected by the Roman Navy.

She would then bypass the southernmost point of the Aegean Sea, before reaching the relative safety of land, the western most point of the Greek Islands.

Unknown to the Captain of the Herculaneum, on the following high tide, two slender trireme's departed from Porto, a small coastal area north of Rome. These trireme's were built for speed. Three rows of oarsmen on each side of the low sitting vessel, designed for speed and stealth.

Within two days they had caught sight of their quarry. The Herculaneum was an imposing, quinquereme, five rows of sweating oarsmen on each side. But she was designed to transport large quantities of cargo, quite often grain. She was big, sturdy and very, very slow.

By the seventh night the Herculaneum was in open sea. The pirate ships, in addition to being fast had one other advantage, a reinforced buttress or ram under the waterline on the bow of the ship.

As night had fallen the oarsmen on the Herculaneum had been reduced to a skeleton crew. She ambled along barely making headway at less than 4 nautical miles per hour.

The pirate galleys were ready. They had pulled ahead, sailing wide of the Herculaneum. The moonless night aiding their subterfuge.

Before long they were ready. One pirate vessel was situated at 10.00 o'clock, one league in front of the Herculaneum, the other at 2.00 o'clock. In unison they both started moving towards the center. The pirate ship sailing with the current was soon closer. As she approached the Herculaneum, she increased her speed, the oars master sounding a gradually quickening beat. The second pirate ship held back, in reserve, in case she was needed.

No one aboard the Herculaneum, was aware of the impending disaster. The bow wave created by the underwater buttress of the pirate ship led the charge. A resounding crunch, penetrated deep amidships. The Herculaneum groaned in protest, almost buckling under the pressure.

As soon as the pirate ship had rammed the Herculaneum the oars master sounded the reverse thrust. At the sound, one hundred and fifty sweating, muscle clad pirates pulled in the opposite direction. Within seconds the Herculaneum groaned again, releasing the buttress of the pirate galley.

Pandemonium broke out aboard the Herculaneum. Crew members ran on deck, but resistance was futile, all aboard the slow moving Quinquereme knew she was going to sink. The only question, resist the pirates and die either by sword, arrow or drowning, or surrender, and live to see another day, albeit not in freedom.

Leading the surrender was Gaius Augustus, confidence and arrogance displayed in every step. He knew that the pirates might kill the entire crew, but the ransom his family would pay for him would guarantee his safety. Displaying remarkable courage, he walked across the deck of the sinking Herculaneum, shouting out across the mild sea,

"I am Gaius Augustus, who is in charge here?"

At first no one answered him, he repeated his call,

"I am Gaius Augustus, who is in charge here?" His voice boomed with confidence across the sea to the decks of the pirate galley.

From the privateer a scruffy toothless scoundrel pushed his way to the front.

"You should be worth a pretty penny." The Pirate challenged Gaius Augustus in a guttural sneer. Gaius Augustus didn't flinch, responding imperiously.

"How much are you going to ransom me for?"

"You should be worth twenty talents of silver." Exclaimed the captain salivating over the extortionate demand he had made. Gaius Augustus, not to be outdone shouted back.

"You ignorant fool, I am worth twice that, in fact my friends will pay 50 talents of silver for my safe return." After staring down his captors, he added,

"Then I'll come back, hunt you down, and crucify every one of you heathens."

The ransom was paid and Gaius Augustus was released. Weeks later, Gaius Augustus, now known as Julius Caesar returned at the head of a Roman fleet. The future master of the Mediterranean captured all of his ex-captors and crucified each and every one.

After Caesar's spectacular revenge on his captors, pirates were hunted down, but Rome spared numerous Cilician pirates.

Those who surrendered were settled in various parts of the Mediterranean, where the population was sparse.

The descendants of some of these cut-throats survive today, practicing the same trade -- trafficking in human misery of all ages. One such descendant is an ex-sailor, the proprietor of a bar of dubious repute in the old port of Marseilles.

CONTENTS

1 MATCH-MAKING

Captain Pedro O'Flynn stood outside the Sea Wolfe bridge looking through his binoculars, his attention riveted on an old tugboat chugging toward his vessel.

The beaten up vessel carried a 20' by 8' by 8' battered container, secured prominently on its main deck. The container was so old and rusted it looked a good fit for the tug, both of indeterminate original color, having lost any semblance of a coat of paint.

O'Flynn frowned, finished his cursory inspection of the tug and lifted the microphone to the boat's communication system.

"This is the Captain speaking. I need a security team on deck in three minutes. Assume defensive positions. Do not open fire unless you get orders from the Raven or myself."

O'Flynn liked to dress in immaculate whites, his Captain's hat worn a little to one side, an exclamation point to his massive arrogance. It was evident to everyone that he thought himself a player –Don Juan himself – but it was an opinion few others shared.

His weathered complexion gave the impression of years at sea. He sported a short, scruffy beard – normally some days old – totally at odds with his immaculate uniform. His smile exuded self-confidence he could not back up and was it a constant irritant to all the other officers on the bridge.

None of the crew understood why the yacht owner had chosen a scoundrel like O'Flynn to captain his pride and joy. Even more confusing was the fact that seemingly out of the blue, the Raven had fired his previous Skipper. No one dared question the master of what was, for an individual entrepreneur, a rather impressive yacht. The Raven hadn't risen through the ranks of the darker side of free enterprise through poor choices, and that included his selection of skippers.

The Sea Wolfe's hull gleamed snow white, making it indistinguishable from the hundreds of other pleasure yachts of the uber wealthy plying the exotic ports in the South of France. She had all the usual luxuries of a mega yacht – a pool, a spa, and a large movie theater titled the d'Isigny room; a galley equipped with the finest food and beverages as well as two five-star chefs; plus luxurious sleeping accommodations. But inside, this extravagant exterior beat the heart of a lion with the military muscle to it back up.

The nerve center of this Trojan horse was a command and control center with state-of-the-art satellite links. The ship was equipped for defensive as well as offensive operations, maintaining a well-trained unit of ex-special forces soldiers from various countries around the world. A missile-detection system and a constantly updated cache of the most sophisticated weapons on the market rounded out her arsenal.

At O'Flynn's summons, three heavily armed commandos ran on deck, led by a six-foot-tall figure in black, the only hint of an identity, a ponytail hanging out from underneath a dark helmet. The Kevlar vest and ammunition belt hid any trace of anatomy.

The commandos were equipped with assault rifles, held in two hands across their chests at the ready. They arrived on the starboard side of the deck, hidden from the view of the tugboat, and the team leader lifted an arm signaling them to hold positions. The leader then raised a hand and signaled one commando to the stern and one to the bow.

Major Monique LeFeu had earned a reputation as rough but effective in the French Foreign Legion. As she entered her position mid-ships, the Captain called her over the ship's comm system.

"Monique, are you ready?"

Her beautiful, somewhat vulnerable eyes turned to stone, her face adopting a look of distrust, as if she had sized up the Captain and found him wanting.

Trying to hide her contempt, she answered, "Captain, if you ever refer to me again by my first name when we are on duty, I will show you why I was kicked out of the Legion."

If there was ever an example of conduct not becoming of an officer, O'Flynn would have been the poster boy. He continued undeterred.

"You never did tell me why you were asked to leave Le Legion Etrangère."

He botched the pronunciation, but still hoped to impress a bored and enraged LeFeu. Then he added "Couldn't keep up with the boys, humhh?"

Thinking himself quite witty, he looked around at his crew, hoping to see their approval. Their looks of hostility were not what he expected. O'Flynn had hardly finished looking over his nearby sailors when the wind was taken completely out of his sail by the answer he received from LeFeu.

"Actually, I castrated my commanding officer."

She paused before continuing, letting him stew in uncertainty. "We had an old score to settle AND he tried to take advantage of me. He was 6-foot-2 and 280 pounds."

O'Flynn was flustered, unable to form an answer. LeFeu enjoyed the silence that signaled his confusion, hesitating only a few seconds before adding,

"You are not even close to 6 feet are you, Captain?"

On the bridge of the Sea Wolfe, all eyes turned to O'Flynn, waiting to hear his reaction. He seemed to visibly diminish in size, realizing he had bitten off more than he could chew.

Stuttering slightly with nervous hesitation, he retorted, "I thought the Legion didn't allow females in their ranks anyhow?" His voice tinged with uncertainty, doing his best to derail the conversation.

"They don't." LeFeu did not elaborate nor give an inch. The look on O'Flynn's face confirmed to those on the bridge that he didn't understand, his brow furrowed, his eyes squinted. After an uncomfortable short silence, he obviously decided he'd better leave the subject alone.

"I see," he responded no less confused and wishing he hadn't opened his mouth. He decided for self-preservation's sake to ask in a more circumspect tone,

"Major, is your team ready?"

"Yes, Captain. You may let the tugboat approach."

***

Pieter Stangl – once again living his life as the Raven – watched the approaching tugboat on one of his monitors while he listened to the conversation between O'Flynn and LeFeu. His face, difficult to read, almost preoccupied, showed little emotion. Momentarily, the ship's comm system interrupted his thoughts, and he looked down to see it was Dr. Lucien Drakul calling from the ship's extensive medical facilities.

"I think you better get down here, sir."

"On my way..." Stangl didn't hesitate; he was almost on his way before he had time to put his coffee cup down.

The most unusual post-delivery modification to the Sea Wolfe consisted of a large hospital ward with extensive surgical and laboratory facilities. In short, it offered a self-contained hospital allowing the vessel's medical team to treat any condition a crew member might suffer.

Stangl stormed into the intensive care unit to see Dr. Drakul standing on the far side of an ICU bed equipped with side rails and elevated so the occupant – a young boy – could look at his visitors without raising his head. Life support and cardiac monitoring equipment surrounded the bed. The boy's eyes were opening and closing as he lapsed in and out of sleep or consciousness.

The doctor, dressed in a white lab coat lifted his patient's wrist, feeling the faint pulse, as if trying to verify what the monitors were telling him.

He looked at his new visitor with sadness on his pale face. His shaggy hairstyle and Labrador eyes gave the impression of someone who took his Hippocratic Oath seriously, his medical responsibilities the core of his whole life.

As he monitored his patient's pulse, he shook his head from side to side, his grieving eyes conveying the worst news a family could ever receive.

"I am sorry, it does not look good, signor; his pulse is very weak." Dr. Drakul put the back of his hand to his patient's forehead and seemed unhappy with what he felt. "His hemoglobin count is getting dangerously low; we need another transfusion."

"How long can he last without a bone marrow transplant?" Stangl feared he already knew the answer. Forty years old and standing 6 feet, 4 inches, he was a good six inches taller than the doctor. His jet black hair, tanned face and hook nose gave him a sinister, intimidating look.

The doctor looked again at the Raven, almost afraid to respond, fearing the impact his answer might have.

"The news is not good, signor. We have been maintaining his condition with umbilical cord blood transfusions, but we need to find a donor with matching genes. He needs a bone marrow transplant. It is the only chance...We have to find a match."

Stangl had a quick fuse, he raised his voice considerably, "I am perfectly well aware of his condition, doctor. I asked you how long does my son have?"

On hearing Stangl's voice, the young boy opened his eyes, looked over at his father, confusion, love and uncertainty in his eyes. With what looked like a super human effort, he rasped weakly, "Pappa, are you angry with me?"

Stangl immediately tore his glance away from Dr. Drakul to look at his son, his eyes melted, but before he could answer, his son's eyes closed again, his head slouching to one side, as if the effort to speak had been too much for him.

Stangl's response was heavy-handed but he did not intend to offend the kindly doctor; nor did he want to upset or worry his sick son, he was simply frustrated with the cards he had been dealt.

As his son fell back into unconsciousness, an overwhelming sense of guilt overpowered him. Stangl begged whatever God might be out there to let his son recover enough so that he could make it up to him.

Dr. Drakul swallowed hard a few times, not in fear but more out of pity for the untenable situation of the man before him.

"A month, perhaps two, if we are very lucky."

Most men, on hearing this news, would have been dejected, devastated. After the life Stangl had lived, the person he had become as the Raven, he was not such a man; to give up easily was not in his nature.

Still, he bridled with suppressed frustration. "Prepare the clinic and lab for more tests. We should have another consignment onboard within the   hour."

2 SAHARA SECRETS

The strange activities surrounding the *Sea Wolfe* and its tugboat rendezvous did not go unobserved. On the other side of the world, Colonel Tom Burke occupied the pilot's chair in front of three large-screen TV monitors at the Eyes of Athena OPs Center in Bethesda, Maryland.

Burke sat behind a team of analysts at their computer stations in front of the three screens. One monitor showed the nondescript tugboat and container and another, the *Sea Wolfe*. The third offered a close-up of the *Sea Wolfe's* bridge and O'Flynn.

Burke's attention was riveted on the monitors as he turned to pick up his phone. "Ari, you better get in here."

It had only taken a short time for Ari Cohen to become one of Athena's most important field operatives. He was Israeli-born – although his mother was British – and had been on "loan" to Athena from the Israeli intelligence service, the Mossad. That arrangement had lingered for nearly two decades.

"On my way, Tom."

Ari was in the break room talking with Secret Service Agent David Gray, also an unofficial agent of the Athena organization. He slapped Ari on the back with a hearty smile. "Don't forget dinner on Sunday. Jade will kill us both if you don't show up!"

Ari gave his best friend a big smile, "What, are you still afraid of your wife?"

"You better believe it, brother! And if you knew what was good for you, you would be too!"

Ari left the room laughing softly. He and Gray had truly been as close as brothers since the first Athena operation, when Ari had joined the organization. That operation brought him to Bethesda full-time. It seemed a lifetime ago since Ari had essentially saved Gray's life. Gray had been pulled into the close-knit Athena circle a decade later, and Ari was grateful his friend had been there to return the life-saving favor a time or two.

Moments later, Ari powered into the OPs center. He was so prompt, Burke still had his hand on the comm system, his knuckles white and taught as his grip betrayed the emotion overtaking him. Ari looked to Burke's face, noting his teeth clamped together tightly, his bulging jaw muscles confirming the strain he was under.

"Tom, what's—" Ari broke off, deciding to wait before he continued, giving his CO a chance to get his adrenalin back under control. They had worked so closely together and earned each other's respect, that although Burke was Ari's superior in a military fashion, he felt comfortable using the Colonel's first name.

Ari didn't have to wait long. Burke turned his glance from Ari to one of his analysts. "Pull up the map showing the route the tugboat has taken."

Ari could tell from Burke's tone of voice that his commanding officer was having a difficult time getting his feelings back under control. He had seen Burke in all kinds of stressful situations before – losing team members, facing diabolical plots to subjugate the American people, working against assassination plots, some successful, some thwarted, but he had never seen his friend so strung out.

The satellite image on the screen changed to a map of Greece, the Ionian Sea and the Port of Kalamata. Burke turned to look at Ari. "This tugboat picked up a container in Kalamata; infrared is indicating 17 children inside."

Ari turned quickly toward Burke, understanding now the reason for the sickly green tint of his skin. "Kalamata..." he said in a tone Burke mistakenly took to be a question, as if Ari didn't know where it was.

"You don't know Kalamata?"

"I do. I'm surprised the little port is big enough to handle containers, I thought they just exported olive oil."

Burke still seethed, but he tried to zero in on the mission. "We have had that place on our radar screen for some time because some of the cruelest Eastern European crime syndicates use that sleepy little port as a gateway to the rest of the world."

"How did you find out about this vessel?"

"Luck really. As you know, we've had the Raven under surveillance for some time – more keeping tabs since he has stayed relatively under the radar after he wiped out half the Chicago mob.

"Anyway, we intercepted a radio transmission with the Raven agreeing to buy a consignment of 17 units of blood type AB. We are still not sure why. What we do know is there appear to be 17 kids in that container. A coincidence wouldn't you say?"

The screen image returned to a close-up of the tugboat. It zoomed in on the name, *Sahara, Algiers*, the plaque so old and worn it was barely visible on the stern. Ari and Burke stared at the screens, puzzled.

"Get me info on the *Sahara's* captain," the Colonel barked.

When Burke shouted an order in the OPs Center, it became a hive of activity. No one, but no one, even thought of questioning his order. The OPs Center was a quiet tornado of flying fingers across keyboards with the analyst staff anxiously seeking the information the CO wanted.

The first analyst to get a hit turned 90 degrees in his swivel office chair and held up his hand to get the CO's attention. "His name is Rafik Taman, an Algerian. The *Sahara* is owned by some Swiss shell company," he announced triumphantly, hoping for some form of recognition for a job well done.

"What's the shell company's name?"

"Oiseaux de Proie. A. G."

Burke hesitated, but only for a millisecond. He looked around the room, as if he were waiting for someone to clarify. He finally focused on Ari, whom he knew would understand.

With a slight shake of his head, breathing out noisily, he uttered, "Team, I'm not a dadgum linguist. I have enough trouble with English."

Looking around, he added,

"What is that in our lingo?"

"Birds of Prey, sir. The AG is synonymous with our incorporated."

"Do you have any more info on this *Taman*?

The same analyst responded, "He's a ghost, sir; nothing on him before assuming control of the *Sahara*. I'll keep looking."

"Humhh... Strange..." He stood silently for a moment, thinking deeply about the new information he had received.

He was slightly startled when Ari spoke beside him. "You were able to pick up a live conversation between the Raven and a third party?"

Burke nodded absently.

"I thought the Raven's communications were always encrypted; why the lapse in protocol?"

Ari and Burke gave one another a knowing glance; they didn't believe in   coincidences.

3 SILENCE AND SHOCK

Off the southern coast of France, within easy sight of the skimpily clad sun-worshippers on the beaches of the Promenade des Anglais in Nice, the *Sea Wolfe* and the Sahara rocked gently on the mirror-like morning waters of the Mediterranean Sea.

As the early beach-goers settled into their rented chaise lounges and prepared for a day of decadence on the fashionable stretch of sand, Stangl sat in his stateroom below the main deck of his yacht, finishing his Cafe au Lait and croissant and watching the proceedings above on a closed-circuit television from a camera posted high above the bridge on the main mast.

With a flick of a button, he sent the monitor gliding back up into the recesses of the ceiling. In his normal, carefully measured gait, he made his way topside.

From the bridge of each boat, the captains watched the progress as their vessels approached each other. The *Sea Wolfe* sat high above the water, giving the impression that O'Flynn, manning the bridge of the taller ship, strained to look down. In fact, he tried to make sure the buoys were deployed correctly as the *Sahara* – every inch a rust bucket – pulled parallel to the *Sea Wolfe* to match her speed.

On the *Sahara*, Skipper Rafik Taman stood outside his bridge, watching the delicate gap between the two ships. He leaned over the side, giving hand signals to his first mate, who manned the helm. When the skipper was sure the boat was where he wanted it, with the distance between the two ships as close to constant as possible, he straightened up and looked to the bridge area of the *Sea Wolfe*.

To the casual observer, it appeared both captains were totally absorbed in their jobs. Closer inspection of Taman would find he was not as focused on the distance between the two boats as he was on O'Flynn.

Taman watched O'Flynn with a mystifying intensity. His eyes narrowed, not from looking up through the bright sun (he was in the shade caused by the proximity of the much larger *Sea Wolfe*) but from the deep furrows on his brow. His mouth clamped shut, the jaw muscles under his ears pulsating as he crunched down hard on his lower jaw. The look on his face could only be explained by some intense emotion – disgust or perhaps jealousy. Whatever it was, it was clear Taman was obsessed with O'Flynn.

No sooner had the lapse occurred than Taman reassumed control over his inner emotions. Gone was the sneer and hatred, replaced by the happy-go-lucky smile of a bored and disinterested skipper, Gauloise hanging lazily out of the side of his mouth.

Taman was again master of his crew, turning his attention to the container. His deck hands began to secure the ropes from the winch as the operator engaged the pulley. As the ropes took up the slack, tiny particles of dust squeezed out to dance in the early morning sunshine.

As the container began to move, the first mate of the *Sahara* looked from the bridge to his skipper. Nodding toward the container, he uttered in a compassionate tone, "I hope they are all right in there."

Taman also nodded his head. "That's why we made the crossing at night and they have water and blankets." As an afterthought, he added, "Steady as she goes there, Mate, maintain that distance."

The container lifted, starting to swing gently on its upward path to clear the deck of the *Sahara*, crossing the water to the *Sea Wolfe*. The winches strained noisily, still lifting the load in order to reach the deck height of the higher vessel. A wave large enough to rock both boats caused the container to jerk abruptly and swing much more wildly. From inside, a hammering sounded like a base drum, ever increasing in volume. Frightened occupants in the container began stamping and banging against the walls.

As soon as O'Flynn saw the container clear the *Sahara's* deck, he called out to his first officer, "Get down on deck. I want the hoses aimed at that container as the doors are opening, just in case... Give them a good clean up, too, before they set foot on my ship."

"Yes, sir."

On the deck of the *Sea Wolfe*, Tony, the first officer, prepared the crew for the arrival of the container. As it crossed the gap between the vessels, over the loud noise of the diesel engine powering the winch, the crew of the *Sea Wolfe* could hear the ruckus coming from inside. As the load started to descend from above the bow of the *Sea Wolfe*, the vibrations from the container affected its balance and the drumming grew louder.

The winch operator aboard the *Sahara* saw the movement − the beginning of a perhaps out-of-control descent − and decided to release the brake. The container accelerated rapidly downward. The deck of the *Sea Wolfe* was immaculate, painted white, not even a spot of rust or dust, and as the container crashed to the deck, two things happened − the hammering from inside the container stopped and a haze of dust-like particles rose from the *Sea Wolfe's* deck.

The first officer had his men waiting, manning two fire hoses in front of the container. Two sailors on each of the 3-inch hoses leaned back in anticipation of the coming onslaught of pressure built up by the water pumps below deck.

"Open the hoses!" Tony shouted.

The sailors securing the fire hoses braced for the sudden surge of pressure, and two more sailors − one on either side of the container − released the lock and pulled open the doors. Major LeFeu and her team approached, assault rifles at the ready, prepared, in case enemies lurked inside, hidden.

All on deck waited, the noise from the powerful hoses drowning out other sounds from the ship. The fire hoses drenched everyone inside. The children, who moments earlier had been hammering on the container walls, screamed in fright, shouting gibberish in their panic.

After verifying there was no threat from inside the container, LeFeu signaled to stop the water cannons, leaving a wet throng of clean but confused children in their wake.

All was quiet as 17 children stared out, dripping wet and standing stock-still. They blinked furiously in the sudden dazzling daylight, watching but not knowing what to expect. Dr. Drakul was beside himself; he came to the front, elbowing past the crew with the fire hoses, clearly agitated.

He shouted to LeFeu, "Is it really necessary to treat these children in this manner?" The doctor's voice conveyed as much anger as he could muster, wrapped in a good dose of indignation.

LeFeu, a 6-foot beauty hiding under her military outfit, shrugged her shoulders guiltily. "I'm sorry, Doctor. The ship's security must come first; we are dealing with some very depraved people. You can have them now and minister to your flock."

Dr. Drakul was still upset. He waved over his medical assistants as he continued toward the container, signaling them to hurry.

From the supplies they were carrying, he grabbed as many towels as he could carry and strode purposefully inside the container to hand them out. He bellowed behind him to no one in particular, "Bring me more towels!"

In no time, all the children were toweling themselves, rubbing the salt water from their hair and their faces, massaging their eyes, which had been irritated by the water and the sudden light. The doctor's gentle tone of voice calmed the terrified children, and his soothing nature, kindly demeanor and grandfatherly, sympathetic eyes soon drew the children to him.

"Come, come," he all but chanted. He stood to one side, making sure the container occupants followed him. Without exception, the children fell into line. As they left the container, wary of their new environment and the sudden intense sunlight, they all tried to get as close as they could to the doctor and as far away as possible from LeFeu and her team of soldiers and water-cannon-wielding sailors.

Dr. Drakul was almost cooing now. He had taken ownership of the children, and, as if he wasn't sure whether they would understand his English, he took hold of a sandwich from the platter a steward held out and pretended to munch on it to show them what he meant.

"Come, come. Take a sandwich, you must be hungry."

At first, there was some hesitation. The suspicious children had stopped, unsure. They looked all around them. For most it was their first time at sea, in fact the first time to see the ocean.

After many seconds, the hunger of one, who tentatively reached forward to snatch a sandwich, led to a stampede of grubby little hands reaching for food. Most even managed a frightened smile, beginning to interact with the kindly doctor. In the midst of the crowd, Dr. Drakul waved the children to follow him, leading them down to the sick bay.

***

Athena Operations Center
Bethesda, Maryland

Athena OPs was silent as all hands, including Ari and Burke, watched the live satellite feed. No one spoke, nervous as the now chattering children were led below decks. There was something unsettling about the scene, the monitors showed various angles of a rusty tugboat sitting alongside a mega luxury yacht, reflecting dazzling morning sunshine off its pristine white decks while a group of undernourished children dressed in rags were led inside for what purpose no one could fathom.

"What do you make of that, Ari?" Burke was the first to break the silence, wrenching his eyes away from the monitors.

Ari hesitated before answering He looked anxious and confused. "I don't like it, Tom. I don't see the Raven."

Ari's glance returned to the images searching for something. "My gut is screaming alarm bells." He hesitated again, still looking at the images above. "There's something bothering me about that officer, almost as if I know her. I can't put my finger on it."

Trying to force the memory, Ari unwittingly walked toward the screens. "Another thing, why are they doing the transfer in broad daylight? The Raven must know we have satellites watching every square inch of the Mediterranean."

"Humhh, Ari." Burke frowned now as well. "That doesn't add up; it's as if they either don't care if they are seen or want to be seen."

They both turned their eyes to the monitors and fell back into deep thought analyzing the situation, frowning, struggling for an answer.

One of the analysts manning a computer station in front of Burke interjected, "Sir, we are about to lose our satellite links. We should be able to hook up again to another satellite in about 20 minutes."

As Ari and Burke watched, the image began to flicker, then went blank. The analyst broke the spell by stating the obvious, "We lost them, sir. I'll work on a new connection."

Ari turned to Burke, having a hard time getting a handle on what he had just seen. "I've got a real bad feeling about this, Tom. Why would a man like the Raven be involved in child trafficking? If you are correct and they are sorting their victims by blood type, that could mean organ harvesting. This is almost too gruesome to contemplate."

Burke sprang into action, booming out with authority, "Staff, I need some intel on underage abduction in and around Kalamata and on to the South of France."

One analyst responded almost immediately. "I've been working on that, sir, and I have a dossier ready for you."

Burke looked at the analyst surprised, staring hard. His team was good, but not that good. He turned toward Ari. Last week, Ari had come to him with news that his niece was missing – from somewhere in France.

"Give it to me, son."

As soon as Burke started reading, he cringed in disgust. His analyst had obviously been impacted by his research as well.

"In Europe, child sex slavery has reached epidemic proportions. What started off as a sideline for some of Europe's less savory criminals has turned into a major business and profit center for some of the world's most ruthless crime syndicates. Child prostitution has turned to smuggling to supply pimps worldwide with a steady source of humiliated, scared children, who are frequently intimidated into cooperating with their captors.

"Beyond trafficking the helpless children and teens for the sexually depraved, other markets exist for child workers and, more importantly, for the harvested internal organs of men, women and children.

"According to the World Health Organization, the trafficking of illegally obtained human internal organs takes unfair advantage of the poorest and most vulnerable groups in society."

No kidding, Burke thought.

"Kidneys are the most trafficked organ, because one can be removed in less-than-hospital-like conditions without the patient losing his or her life.

"A frequent tactic of these syndicates is to kidnap children of illegal aliens worldwide. These most vulnerable members of society are then blackmailed into working for or cooperating with the crime syndicates under threat of exposure of their families.

"Many of these children are at first employed as sex slaves, and when their usefulness in this industry is at an end, they are sold off to the gangs that handle organ harvesting. At this stage, children are quite often killed for all of their organs, which are harvested simultaneously.

"The WHO estimates nearly 7,000 kidneys are illegally trafficked annually, netting more than $1 billion each year."

Burke looked up from the report to the screen before them, worry etched on his face. He handed the sheet to Ari.

"A recent report from Great Britain has revealed that the first case of a child being trafficked into Britain for the express intention of providing organs for people desperate for a transplant. The girl, whose identity has been protected, was taken from Africa and smuggled into the UK so that her organs could be removed and sold.

"A British government report revealed human trafficking has reached record levels, rising by 50 percent in the last year. Of the cases the government has discovered, and more than 300 have been investigated, most show signs they were sexually abused. Most of the victims came from Vietnam, with some from Nigeria, China, Romania and Bangladesh.

"According to the World Health Organization an international shortage of organs for transplantation has led to a black market for organ trading, as well as organ transplant tourism.

"Transplant tourism?" Burke said incredulously. "What in the Sam hill is that?"

"People of means who need transplants and would otherwise be on waiting lists for years are traveling to third world countries where high-end facilities perform the transplant surgeries with these purchased organs, sir."

Burke and Ari shared a look, and Burke simply shook his head and went back to the report.

"Our investigation turned up an informant in Europe who provided documentation. These organizations, on a worldwide basis, have started to maintain a digital profile on all victims in their syndicates. Preliminary investigation indicates this data not only includes blood type and profile, but also detailed DNA profiles.

"According to WHO spokesman Edward Brooks-Smith, if this information is confirmed, it is a terrifying development, leading authorities to believe these crime syndicates are now operating an organ-harvesting-on-demand business that victimizes the world's most innocent and vulnerable citizens."

Burke handed the remaining page to Ari and all but fell into the pilot's chair. He had spent years in the espionage game and time in the military before that. He thought he had seen the worst people could do to one another, but whenever children were involved … and now this …

His mind refused to process the ramifications of what he had just read. All eyes in the OPs Center were on Burke as he finished reading the report. After a moment, he pulled a handkerchief from his pant pocket and commenced to clean the reading glasses he had just taken off. Not a word was said, the atmosphere in the OPs center heavy; even the analysts sitting at their stations were quiet and apprehensive. Beside him, Ari let the last page fall to the desk top.

Finally, Burke looked up, opening his mouth as if to say something. He took the time to look around the room and eyeball each member of his staff individually. No one spoke; Burke just masticated his lips together. After a few seconds communicating non-verbally with each person, he finished by looking at Ari.

Burke's mind was spinning. This was a situation so far removed from normal operating parameters that he was unsure how he would justify the course of action he was now determined to take.

Slowly a smile spread across his face as he realized the founding fathers of the Eyes of Athena had created this organization for exactly this reason, so that Athena could act without waiting on politicians to justify a wrong against children. Justifying it further to himself, he surmised that innocent children in this country would also be victimized if he didn't do something.

As Burke's face turned to a smile, so did Ari's.

Ari was the first to break the silence. In a voice tight with emotion, he asked, "Can we follow the children and mount a rescue operation when they arrive in port?"

"That's the least we can do." Burke knew Ari was thinking of his young niece. She had disappeared from a store in Paris when she wandered away from her mother. No ransom had been asked, and the police had no leads, unsure if she was really taken or had simply run away.

Ari and his family knew she would have never left on her own. Renee could be anywhere, perhaps kidnapped. The uncertainty – not knowing whether she was alive, dead or compromised – was destroying her family. *She could be among those 17 children*, Ari thought, looking up to the screen. Hope, any slight chance of getting her back, of saving her, was all Ari asked.

***

Aboard the *Sea Wolfe* in the Raven's Stateroom

Stangl paced the length of his stateroom. He stopped in front of a painting hanging on the wall behind his desk. He had commissioned the work nearly a decade ago after he learned the truth about his parents.

Ambassador Graham Martin, his signature cigarette in his hand, eyes hidden behind dark sunglasses, stood stubbornly facing out beyond the walls of the American Embassy, steadfast in his refusal to leave the grounds. Behind him, a helicopter evacuated personnel on a makeshift helipad. Another, larger Huey waited its turn to land just beyond. Lines of evacuees waited anxiously to board the rescue choppers D.C. had sent.

The bronze plaque under the painting read simply, *U.S. Military Evacuation, Saigon, Vietnam, April 28, 1975.*

It always moistened his eyes, knowing at that very moment, his parents, Alex and Heidi Stangl, had signed their death warrants to save him and his brother, Wolfgang. Their only crime – his mother did not have a U.S. passport.

They had placed their twin newborns into the hands of strangers to be evacuated. His father had worked for the CIA, but he wouldn't leave their mother behind. They had escaped the Embassy grounds only to drown trying to get to the ships outside the harbor.

He stared at the painting now, as he did whenever he had a difficult decision to make or faced a task weighing heavily on him. In spite of his sadness, it gave him a great strength of purpose, reminding him of his parents' sacrifice and the knowledge that in the most extreme of situations, there is always a solution.

Stangl racked his brain, looking for a solution for his son; he refused to admit defeat. Ever since his briefing with Dr. Drakul in the intensive care ward, he had felt utterly helpless. His knew his son was dying, the chances of finding a match 10,000 to 1.

He turned from the painting to a photo on his desk. His wife, Jade, stared out of the frame, his tiny son in her arms. The Sicilian Mafia had taken her from him when Theo was just an infant. If it hadn't been for Lannie, he would have lost Theo, too. Anger cast a dark hue across his eyes. He had found Jade in the midst of his renewal – a new life in Vietnam, where it had all started. Together, they took in Lannie – a kid off the streets – and had then been blessed with Theo.

He had broken ties with the mafia, thinking he had paid the dues they required for his freedom, but they had come, and his beautiful wife was gone. Now, not even a decade later, he could lose their son. He had never been a man of great faith – he left that to Lannie – but there were times when he believed there was a God and that God hated him.

His morbid thoughts and guilt were interrupted by the phone ringing, and he almost jumped over the desk in his hurry to hear the news. He already knew who would be calling.

That was the reason for his latest odyssey – a quest to save his son's life and correct an injustice. The phone beeped urgently now, almost before Stangl had the handset to his ear.

"Sir, we have one possible genetic match, looks like 75 percent."

Stangl knew that a 75 percent match was still a 5,000 to 1 shot, but even so it was a chance. The *Sea Wolfe* was one of the most luxurious yachts on the open sea, but his stateroom was still not tall enough to allow him to jump and imitate a slam dunk. If it were, that was precisely what he felt like doing.

"Good work, doctor!" Stangl literally screamed in jubilation, turning to look at his painting again, and mouthing a silent thank-you, a smile spreading across his face.

On the other end of the phone, Dr. Drakul abruptly tore the phone away from his ear as Stangl's elation rocketed down the phone line making his eardrums bristle.

"Make that child as comfortable as possible. Send the rest up on deck; they probably need some fresh air."

As he hung up the phone, Stangl suddenly felt guilty for his thoughts of only moments before and humbled with gratitude. All his life, all he had ever asked for, hoped for, was a shot, a chance to beat the odds. Whether it was his parents looking down on him from a Heaven he hoped existed or the God who seemed just beyond the grasp of his belief, he was overwhelmed.

He paused a moment, thinking, *Can you call it prayer if it was just a bunch of lonely nights full of tearful begging to a God you're unsure of?* He shrugged. *If so, this was a prayer answered.*

He smiled as he turned toward the comm system. As he did he thought, *This must be it. God, the Universe, whatever – nothing could be so cruel as to bring success almost within reach again, only to have the rug pulled out from under me.*

As he waited for the captain to answer his call, his mind wandered to another problem he would have to find an answer for soon.

How will I handle Captain Pedro O'Flynn? Stangl had offered him so much money to join his crew that O'Flynn couldn't resist – even if it meant his old employer might want to hunt him down.

Before he could contemplate his own question anymore, he heard the Captain answer his summons, "O'Flynn."

Stangl was brief. "Prepare to make way, Captain. Make sure Taman gets rid of the container."

"Yes, sir. Where to?"

"To Poros; we don't have a lot of time."

O'Flynn had been born in the ghettos of Naples, the illegitimate son of an Irish sailor and an Italian whore. His birth had never been registered, his early childhood scarred by the street life prevalent to many poor urchins in Naples.

His father tried to be a positive influence on young Pedro in those early years, wanting the boy to carry his family name. But when he had to go back to sea, O'Flynn's mother returned to the only life she knew that would put food on their table.

O'Flynn was left to his own devices most of the time in an area overrun with violent crime and influenced by powerful criminal organizations. Drug trade and gang feuds were common in this area of high unemployment and filth, and it was natural for O'Flynn to turn to the crime syndicate for his own protection.

It wasn't long before he became a runner for the syndicate. Businesses, shopkeepers and craftsmen in these regions were expected to pay protection money to syndicate families controlling their areas. This was where he excelled. Those trying to escape payment were forced to deal with O'Flynn, always backed up by his gang of young enforcers.

Many of the other gang enforcers used intimidation, threatening to break windows and steal inventory. O'Flynn was more creative; he kidnapped family members – wives and children – and in little time, he had the most productive route in the criminal enterprise, rising quickly through the ranks.

As the syndicates' business interests grew, and human trafficking became a profit center too lucrative to ignore, they sent Pedro off to Holland and The Royal Naval College, the academy of the Royal Netherlands Navy. He spent five long years there. Upon completion of the program, he was awarded a bachelor's degree, and instead of being commissioned in the Royal Netherlands Navy, his employers "arranged" for him to be returned to the syndicate to captain their fledgling maritime transportation division. The education gave him a sense of respectability – at least on paper.

***

Athena Operations Center
Bethesda, Maryland

Everyone in the Athena OPs room waited breathlessly for the new satellite to come into position. There was no happy banter during the wait; time dragged on. Although they all had numerous digital devices to check the time, it seemed everyone's eyes were glued to the clocks hanging on the wall between monitors.

The local time, as well as in London, Moscow and Hong Kong, was displayed prominently in front of everyone. Every second took an eternity to pass, and depression hung over the room like a blanket of fog. Most could not remove the horrific scenes of human depravity their imaginations had conjured up during the interminable wait to regain access to the satellite signal.

Their worst fears of cruelty and horror, a torture beyond understanding, had everyone praying that what they suspected could not possibly be true.

Finally, a satellite began to come into range, a monitor started to come online, and momentarily, all screens were flickering. Suddenly, they burst into life, startling the watchers with the sudden clarity of the bow deck of the *Sea Wolfe*.

Simultaneously, all hands in the OPs center assumed a rigid posture, craning their necks to see as much as they could. One by one, children began to emerge from below decks, those in front lifting their hands to their foreheads to try to shade their eyes from the sudden, intense sunlight. Ari counted them to himself as they appeared.

An analyst working the bank of monitors in front of Burke let out another alarm. "Sir, our window on this interim satellite is going to close in 20 seconds; our satellite will be coming into range in two minutes."

The image began to flicker and fade again, the screens lost their connection. Anxiety in the control room mounted.

Ari turned to Burke and, almost as if afraid to verbalize what his eyes were telling him, he said in a near-whisper, "I only counted 16 coming back on deck, I think... I think one of them is missing."

There was nothing to say, the OPs center returned to deathly silence again, the only sound, one analyst nervously clicking a ball point pen. The more he clicked, the more people began to look at him. After a short while he felt the weight of all eyes on him, as if the frustration everyone felt was turned his direction. He looked quickly around the room, then realized the cause of everyone's' irritation and threw the pen on his desk as if it were a poisonous insect.

Suddenly a hopeful voice boomed out, "One minute, sir."

The Athena satellite link was re-established; the monitors burst into life showing the brilliant summer sun shining on the filthy squalor of the container, a stark contrast to the gleaming deck of the Raven's yacht.

All eyes in the OPs center watched as the satellite view on the monitors panned in on the container, only to see the doors of the container being re-bolted closed. For a few seconds the control room was silent, everyone scanning the monitors for any sign of the children. Different views from the satellite scanned around the deck, only the lee side of the deck invisible.

"Did anyone see where the children went?" Burke bellowed, knowing it was a rhetorical question. Everyone in the OPs center could only see the same monitors, the same video he did.

In spite of that knowledge, he asked again, "Are they inside the yacht or in the container?"

Burke looked around the OPs center, as if hoping a member of his team might have divine knowledge of what occurred. Ari was beside himself, shrugging his shoulders in a very continental gesture of having no answer.

"I don't know." In contrast to Burke's thunderous question, Ari's voice was faint, but no one in the OPs center interpreted it as anything other than a viper coiled in rage.

All eyes in the room were glued to the monitor as the container slowly lifted off the deck of the *Sea Wolfe* and swung back toward the *Sahara*. All was silent.

"The container seems heavy, sir. Could be the water they used to wash it down or..."

"That's not what I wanted to hear, team."

After an excruciatingly slow and tension-filled crossing, the container touched down on the deck of the *Sahara*. The crew ran forward to unhitch the shackles.

All eyes watched as the tugboat, with container on board, hit reverse thrust, slowly separating from the yacht. As the distance widened, the tug resumed a forward direction, turning back toward land and it's destination.

"Looks like the tugboat is heading west-northwest. Do we have any assets in the Eastern Mediterranean?" Burke asked.

"Checking now, Colonel."

Only one analyst, Simon, watched the monitors. Ari and Burke were huddled over a table examining a map of the Mediterranean, trying to pinpoint where the *Sahara* might be headed. Simon swallowed hard, not able to believe what his eyes saw. After a few moments, his worst suspicions were confirmed and he turned to get Burke's attention.

"Sir, Ari, You gotta see this!" He turned back to the monitor, as the others also turned to look at the satellite images.

"Oh, no! I don't, no! I don't— Look!" Simon did not need to explain further. The urgency conveyed in his voice at a fever pitch had been enough to get everyone to look at the revelation on the screen in front of them.

It only took Ari, Burke and the other analysts a few seconds to realize what was happening. The *Sahara* had pulled away from the *Sea Wolfe* heading due west, her stern bathed in the rising sun, her wake thundering out behind her, like an upside down Niagara Falls. The *Sea Wolfe* was disappearing in the distance when the *Sahara* stopped making headway. Sailors approached the container, connecting winch lines to the chassis at the bottom. As soon as all lines were secured, a sailor on deck turned toward the bridge to give the thumbs-up sign to the winch operator to engage.

Rust-colored dust was ejected from the metal cable as the lines took up the slack. Every face in the Eyes of Athena OPs center frowned, no one understanding what the crew was doing. With a groan, the container started moving again. Slowly at first, only one end attached by cable, the other end scraped along the deck as the arm of the winch struggled to move the massive box toward the port side.

The winch operator maneuvered the controls so the container inched up as it slid closer to the sea. On one monitor in the Athena OPs center, the stern of the *Sea Wolfe* could just be made out in the distance, by now going at full speed, the disturbance churned by the wake hardly visible as she disappeared over the horizon.

Burke watched the image of the *Sahara*, his attention riveted on the container. Unsure of what he was seeing, he asked Simon, "Are they raising the container?"

The question hung in the air unanswered as everyone tried to work out what they were seeing.

"But why?" Momentarily, he was able to answer his own question.

"Oh, by all that is holy... I don't believe it; are they dumping the container overboard?" Burke looked frantically at Ari, so overcome with fear and dread as he spoke that he reached over to grab Ari's arm. Ari winced at the iron-clad grip, although Burke was unaware he was squeezing so hard.

Burke raised his voice a pitch further, asking what no one knew the answer to. "Are the children back in the container or not?"

The container was now at a 45-degree angle, the sailor on the tugboat deck signaled the winch operator with a thumbs-up to swing the elevated side of the container over the sea. The container swung wildly. By now, the captain of the *Sahara* was down on deck supervising the work himself. The bright sunlight was shining directly on his face, enabling the satellite to see that he was a tall, shaggy brute with a scar spanning the length of his face. He signaled with his hand across his throat to the winch operator.

The operator released the line, and the container splashed into the sea. Taman turned to the tugboat bridge, starting to climb up toward his domain with not even a backward glance.

In the Athena OPs Center, shocked, painful silence fell again and Burke finally released his grip on Ari's arm. Ari, momentarily distracted by the pain, shook his arm in relief, before returning his attention to the matter at hand.

All hands watched the monitors with horror as the container began to take on water, sinking slowly below the surface of the sea.

The OPs Center was deathly still as the satellite image moved in for a close-up view of where, just moments before, the container had sunk below the surface. Only air bubbles rose to the surface to break the mirror-like calm of the water. It was too much for Simon; overcome with emotion, he ran out of the room with a handkerchief held over his face, trying to choke back the swell of emotion caused by what he had just seen.

Burke had never seen Ari so angry as he walked over to the remaining analysts sitting in front of the computer monitors. Spitting out in rage and enunciating each word with added emphasis, he said, "Track. That. Tugboat! I want to know where it goes."

Ari turned to Burke, speaking vehemently but with great restraint, doing his best to control the fury he felt and pleading with his eyes.

"Tom, I have to go. One of those kids could be my niece. My sister has called me every night since her little girl, Renee, was taken in Paris... I have to try."

4 WELCOME TO THE BLACK CAT

Marseilles, South Coast of France

The Port of Marseilles dates back to ancient Roman times. The small sub-district where sailors have for centuries sought work, wine and female company lay east of Marseilles toward Callelongue. Wedged between the old fish market and a brothel frequented by lonely sailors for hundreds of years, sits the Black Cat. No sign or billboard advertised its presence, and local authorities stayed away, preferring to let its customers police themselves.

Across the street, behind the entrance to the fish market, Ari stood motionless, watching and waiting in the shadows. He had not shaved for three days, his hair was disheveled, and his short coat was deliberately scuffed and dirty.

As patrons arrived across the street, he aimed his phone's camera, took a picture and hit send. He waited patiently for confirmation, looking for the tugboat captain, Rafik Taman.

No guards manned the massive wooden door where men entered at their own risk. The smell of Turkish tobacco, pastis and sweat permeated the air. Only locals and sailors who had been referred to the Black Cat ventured across the cobbled stone streets to heave open the door.

Due to the dubious business activities of many of its customers, the Black Cat's priest's hole remained a useful amenity. Unseen and unknown by most, it sat above the heavy wooden door, and from that vantage point, a lookout could see up and down the street, as well as across the street to the fish market.

A good many of the Black Cat's customers were happy to pay a little extra for the comfort of knowing they would be warned in the event unwelcome officials or rival gangs came calling. On most nights, Shorty manned the priest's hole. He was of a diminutive stature, but had the eyes of a hawk.

Little did Ari know that Shorty was on duty protecting the clientele, the distant happy banter coming from the bar's customers in the room below a soothing backdrop to his sometimes monotonous vigil. But this night was different; he was about to earn his wage.

***

In the distance, Shorty watched someone near the fish market until he decided it was time to alert his boss. In the room below, friendly conversation was interrupted by a ringing bell over the bar loud enough to get the attention of every customer. As soon as it sounded, the mood was broken. Immediately, silence descended like a heavy blanket over the jovial laughter of patrons.

Louie, proprietor of the Black Cat, was a heavyset, middle-aged ex-sailor with an anchor tattooed on each forearm. He wore a tank top that had seen better days and a week-old beard topped by a lit Gauloise hanging out of his mouth. When the bell rang, he finished drying the glass over which he had been laboring and leaned back against the bar wall to pull out an old speaking tube and mouthpiece used aboard ships for many years.

Pulling it down to his mouth, he bellowed, "What is it, Shorty?"

Louie put the device to his ear to hear, "We have a visitor watching the front door from the fish market."

"Gendarme?"

"No, not local neither. I'll ring the bell again if he makes for the entrance."

In the fish market, Ari continued his patient vigil, gently tapping his feet on the wet concrete against the cold, thinking that if he didn't get out of there soon he would never be able to wash off the stink of old fish. Even the breeze coming from the Mediterranean wasn't able to dull the stench or lighten his mood. The damp, wet, overcast day added to his feeling of foreboding. *Could my niece be here, could she possibly be one of the victims of this operation?*

Another patron approached the Black Cat. Ari stopped trying to warm his feet, strained his senses and his eyes and tried to identify the new arrival. Unsure, he snapped a photo and hit send on his cell phone.

As the figure strode on to the Black Cat, Ari waited for an identification from Athena. Momentarily, his cell phone vibrated. He looked down to read the text message:

"Positive ID. TAMAN. Extremely dangerous."

Ari stepped outside the fish market, stopped to look around, trying to see if he was being watched and then walked toward the bar, pulling up his coat collar against the cold wind. He was about 100 paces behind Taman, who had just opened the door to the Black Cat.

Inside the tavern, as Taman entered and closed the door behind him, the bell rang again, signaling that Shorty had something to report. Louie made a grab for the mouthpiece. "What is it?" he shouted angrily.

"He's on his way."

Louie replaced the device and turned toward Taman.

The skipper of the *Sahara* could feel the tension his entrance had caused, but he was puzzled. Slowly he turned around, at first looking over his shoulder, then to face everyone. As he glanced at each table, he saw they were watching him. Next, he looked behind the bar to see Louie drying a wine glass. The glass was already dry, the barkeep's motions causing a faint high-pitched singing whine, but his eyes betrayed the barman's real focus; they were glued to Taman.

Slowly most of the other guests inspecting Taman returned to their conversations. He was mystified as to the reaction his entrance had caused. The bell sounded again, louder this time, more insistent. Louie waved Taman over. "Quick come up to the bar, we have an uninvited guest approaching."

Louie turned to his other customers and shouted loud enough for all to hear. "Remember, everyone," he said, trying to make eye contact with every person in his bar, "don't do anything to him until we find out who he is and what he wants."

Taman slid up to the bar, doing as he was told. He pulled out an old worn bar stool to sit down while Louie pulled him a draft beer. When the beer was topped off, Louie scrapped the head level with a small wooden spatula, then slid the glass down the bar toward Taman. The frothy head of the beer only dribbled down the rear of the glass as Taman stopped its forward progress.

Before he could savor his fresh brew, the door opened and another whoosh of cold night air invaded the Black Cat. Ari entered the bar, closed the door behind him and stood innocently stamping his feet, hoping the stench of rotten fish was not too obvious. The stony silence in the bar was unmistakable. It wasn't as if the conversation had suddenly stopped, it was as if there was no chatter to begin with. That he was expected was as obvious to Ari as the fishy aroma of his clothes.

Ari opened his coat, flipping his collar down and tried to buy some time to figure out whether he was in immediate danger or not. Slowly, it seemed conversation resumed in the tavern. He glanced around the room pretending to look for a seat. In fact, he was trying to assess where the biggest danger might come from in the event he was attacked.

His recon revealed only one table that caused him concern. Two middle-aged sailors couldn't hide their interest in Ari. They were seated with their feet slightly to the side of their chairs, their hands spread out firmly on the tabletop, as if just waiting on an order to launch themselves toward him.

After a moment, he determined he was in no immediate danger; no one but the two sailors seemed to be paying him much attention. A few guests looked up lazily, most pretended not to even notice him.

Ari looked over at the crowded bar and saw a stool next to Taman. Thinking that location was as good as any, he walked over to claim it. While he was getting comfortable, the bartender walked over.

The French language has many nuances and idiosyncrasies, one of which is the ability to use one word in such a fashion as it could have more than one meaning. Louie's greeting was not cordial; with a sneer, he said, "Monsieur?"

Ari realized he was being asked two things at the same time: "What do you want to drink?" and "What the heck are you doing here?"

He was by now settled at the bar, elbows wedged firmly in front of him. Ari enjoyed this game, confronting a ruffian who thought he held all the cards. Slowly – as insolently as possible and trying to give Louie every impression that he thought the man a low life – Ari looked over at him.

Ari was, in fact, deciding whether Louie was a simple barman or something else. As he finished his assessment, he moved his hand to cup his chin and lightly tapped his forefinger to the side of his jaw. *Not a simple barman,* he concluded. It had only taken a moment to size the man up, and Ari answered, "Rouge, s'il vous plait."

Louie, with a dramatic flourish threw his glass drying towel over his left shoulder, reaching for a glass, and began filling it with red wine. The entire time, he kept his eyes on Ari. When he finished, he passed the glass over to the stranger, but Louie was not through; his "guest" had not answered the second inferred question. Like a bulldog with a bone, Louie was not giving up. In typical French fashion, without taking the Gauloise out of his mouth, he asked simply,

"Americain?"

Ari took stock of his appearance wondering what would possibly give the barkeep that impression. He carried his father's coloring, dark hair and eyes, although his mother had given him slightly finer features. He purposely had no real accent to his speech, and when he was dressed to his normally impeccable standards, he was always thought to be

European. Perhaps it was his hobo's rags and the smell of fish.

He looked at Louie, nodding his head slightly, not in answer to the man's question, but more in affirmation to himself that he had been right; this guy could be a rough customer. Ari resorted back to English, not wanting anyone to know the extent to which he understood French.

"Yeah, sort of."

Louie did not retreat; he maintained his ground, thinking of the next question he wanted to ask, while Ari was thinking he needed to put a finish to this line of questioning.

Before he could think of a way to do it, Louie continued his barrage. "Dangerous place to hang out...the Port of Marseilles."

Taman sat next to Ari at the bar, and no matter how absorbed in his own thoughts he might have appeared to be, he couldn't help noticing as the tone of the conversation between Ari and Louie deteriorated. Nevertheless, he pretended not to pay any attention. In Ari's opinion, he was unnaturally disinterested.

Ari was determined not to give an inch, and decided to answer Louie's last statement. "For some." He volunteered no more than that.

Louie became more aggravated; he wanted to know who this new customer was. As Louie seemed to be making no progress with his "polite" inquiries, he decided to cut to the chase. "What do you want here?"

Ari shrugged, deeming to respond in kind. "I came in for a drink, not conversation."

Louie's face turned cold and the buzz of noisy conversation around them abruptly ended. Other customers decided to stop their game of pretending not to be interested in the stranger. They, too, turned to pay attention to the conversation between Ari and Louie.

Ari noticed the strained look from the barman and decided to mix it up a bit. "Actually, I came in to have a drink with my good friend, Rafik."

Taman was snake bit; he had not been expecting to have the conversation turn in his direction. He had been sitting next to Ari, leaning away from him and trying to distance himself as much as possible from the altercation that seemed unavoidable. He secretly prayed this unexpected meeting between the American and Louie would not blow his cover.

Taman and his boss had spent months developing his new identity. Determined to learn more about child trafficking, Stangl had developed a plan to plant his most trusted employee, the captain of his prized possession the *Sea Wolfe*, undercover. It was a tremendous blow to Taman's ego to swap the captain's quarters on the *Sea Wolfe* for a flea-bitten bunk on the *Sahara*, even as skipper of the rust bucket.

What eventually persuaded Taman to agree to the crazy scheme was intel he had discovered. Through some of his Navy contacts, he learned that Pedro O'Flynn, a high-ranking syndicate enforcer, had been trained to sail on the syndicate's dime. His usefulness tripled as part of the European smuggling operation. The syndicate was quite happy to own an adequate sea captain with a ruthless heart, and he had quickly become a key element in the transportation of their most profitable commodity from Europe – human beings.

But rumor had it that Interpol, the European Secret Police, were hot on his trail, so O'Flynn needed an out. He wanted desperately to disappear from his high-risk illegal activities. If the Raven could snag him, it would be an intel scoop. Once O'Flynn was in the Raven's employ and freely trading his secrets for a captain's luxury stateroom and security, Taman had agreed to take on a new identity and a new life, be it in a flea-ridden tugboat.

He was not ready to have that hard-won cover blown. Ari's comment came as such a surprise that Taman did a double-take. He lifted his head, trying to focus his eyes on Ari. Looking down his nose in a gesture of *What the heck just happened?*

All he could think of to say was, "Huh?"

Ari turned to confront the look on Taman's face. "I hear you like to drop containers overboard at sea."

Now Ari had Taman's full attention. His reaction was sudden and violent; he jumped up from his bar stool, pushing it back. The stool cascaded head over heels behind him, while at the same time, Louie looked over at two of his regulars down at the other end of the bar and gave them a nod. The henchmen rose, armed with heavy truncheons.

Ari followed Louie's line of sight and saw the thugs approaching. He hastily rose, backing toward the door but keeping his eyes on all the potential threats in the bar. In front of the door, Ari crouched low, not only to diminish his size as a target in case the thugs had a gun, but also to ready himself, muscles coiled to launch himself at the first attacker.

Louie watched Ari back up to the door with an evil look on his face. Ari saw Louie's mischievous grin, wondering why. Louie's face turned from a grin to a malicious smile in a fraction of a second, as if … Ari cocked his head frantically looking around him. *What am I missing? Why is he so sure he has me at a disadvantage?*

Ari didn't have to wait long; he followed Louie's eyes down to his own feet as the floor flew from under him. His arms flew out trying to grip anything, flailing wildly, as he disappeared from sight. Only a trap door remained swinging where his feet had been just seconds before.

Unseen by Ari, in the bar above, Louie reached over and grabbed Ari's glass of red wine to swig it down in one gulp. "Merde …Americain..."

***

Inside the Black Cat Bar

Louie paced from one end of the bar to the other. As he passed the center point, he reset the lever he had pulled to send Ari to an unceremonious dumping in the pit below and the trap door closed. On the other side of the bar, the two thugs Louie had summoned returned to their table, but Louie was visibly angry. He tried to figure out the best course of action, knowing he had another batch of children down in the holding cell, next to the rock pit the stranger had been dropped to.

Could the authorities or Interpol have been alerted he was a link in the underground smuggling operation? Louie tried to answer, hammering his right fist into his left palm anxiously. *Who else knew they helped the Russian Bratva smuggle kidnapped men, women and children out of Europe?*

Louie cursed under his breath; he had a bad feeling. Ever since that syndicate man O'Flynn had disappeared, he was nervous, and no one would tell him what had happened to the fool. *Did Interpol get him? Had he turned state's evidence? Was he even now ratting on his former syndicate friends in order to get a lighter sentence?*

Louie needed answers and needed them now. The only person who could answer them was undoubtedly unconscious in the pit below. *But,* he thought, *the stranger seemed to act as if he knew Taman. Was he the loose link? Everywhere I turn I see suspects, but I'll start there, see if Taman knows something.*

He turned to look at Taman with a menacingly cruel snarl on his face. Taman had been dreading this moment. Ever since Ari asked him about dumping the container at sea, he had been stupefied. His first question, *How did he know who I am?* And the second, *How the heck did he know about the container?*

Taman sipped his beer; he couldn't remember one tasting so stale. No matter which way he approached those questions, no answer came to him, which also meant he didn't know how to answer Louie. Looking up, he realized he had run out of time.

"So, Taman, who is your new friend?" Louie demanded. The barman paused to light another Gauloise while Taman sat baffled, shrugging his shoulders.

"I have no clue; I have never seen him before. I don't even know him."

Louie hesitated, took a deep drag on his freshly lighted cigarette, and exhaled forcibly, blowing the smoke into Taman's face. The skipper didn't flinch although his jawline tensed considerably, indicating he was not accustomed to taking this kind of abusive questioning.

"Ah, but he seems to know you." Taman just shrugged again. "Judging from the way he answered your questions, he seems to know a little about you, too. He was none too helpful, don't you think?" Taman said nonchalantly.

Louie grew more agitated. "If I find out that you have betrayed me, I will put you out of business! In fact, I'll put you out...permanently. You get my drift huhhh?"

Louie turned away from Taman to walk over to the side of the bar closest to his henchmen. As he strutted over, he assessed his situation; if the authorities raided his place and found the children, his life wouldn't be worth a plugged nickel. The Bratva would put a contract out on him immediately. Louie glared at Jacques and Henri. Feeling his intense focus on them, they stopped their conversation and turned to Louie who jerked his head to indicate they should come to the bar.

Jacques and Henri knew their boss well; they moved quickly. Louie wasted no time on pleasantries. Looking at Jacques, he growled, "When the tide comes in and wakes our guest, take Henri down to the pit. I want to know what he knows. I need to find out if anyone sent him here. Do what you have to..."

***

Underneath the Black Cat – The Pit

Ari lay unconscious, spread eagled at the bottom of a slimy, rock-walled pit under the Black Cat. His aching body urged him to sleep, but something kept trying to wake him, probing into his subconscious. It was almost as if it knocked on his brain, telling him his rest was over.

As much as he tried to ignore the signals, his senses gradually pierced through his body's defenses, making him aware he was wet, cold and lying uncomfortably on a jagged, hard surface with a grade-one headache tormenting him. Something inside him forced one eye open.

A miniature ecosystem appeared in front of his face as seawater swirled within inches of his eyes and greenish saltwater vegetation tickling his nose.

It must be a nightmare; I must be dreaming. His brain forced his eye muscles to work, separating his eye lids just enough to see movement. *It isn't seaweed tickling my nose*, he realized, *it a teeny weeny crab scampering through the seaweed looking for food.*

Ari jerked up, lifting his head just enough to focus on the crab. "Ahhhh," he groaned to himself, immediately regretting the sudden movement as a jackhammer upgraded his headache from grade one to a nuclear explosion. Rather than sink down and lay prone again, he leaned up on one elbow, trying to use his other hand to tighten a grip on his forehead. The pain was so intense it felt as if his head was going split in two. He gripped harder, trying to make the incessant battering of his brain go away.

Hesitantly, he cranked open his eyes again to sneak a peek between his fingers. As he did so, his tongue made a round of his mouth, not only feeling a suede-like film over his teeth, but also a salty residue. He forced his tongue out to lick his upper lip. "Yuck, sea water and diesel."

Ari looked around. He noticed the sound of water seemed to gurgle through a restricted space nearby. Below him, down a gently sloping grade and at the seemingly lowest point of his rock enclosure, was a cast iron, locked grate, circular in shape, about the size of a manhole cover. Seawater was ebbing back and forth through the grate, and as it did so, a colony of slimy green seaweed danced to and fro in majestic rhythm, keeping time perfectly with the ebb and flow of the sea water.

Reality came crashing back to Ari with the thundering power of an avalanche, overwhelming his subconscious. At the forefront of the barrage of images was the bartender who had got the better of him. *Son of a Gun! A trap door; talk about cliché and old-hat – worse than a sucker punch – but I bloody well fell for it.*

With the reality of his new predicament front and center, a sense of urgency overcame Ari. He looked up to inspect the rest of his new surroundings. Slimy, dark, rock walls made up the pit and were covered in vegetation, barnacles and black mussels. His sense of smell started to work overtime, bringing him the scents of the salty, dense, decaying kelp, tinged with a good dose of manmade pollution, something akin to diesel and dead fish. Crabs meandered around the base of the walls in the watery seaweed sludge, and the walls looked slippery.

The recon of his cell brought back intense pain in his head. Ari tried harder to focus, every second bringing more clarity to his situation. He looked again at the mussels and vegetation that lined the lower part of the pit walls, realizing it must mean seawater flooded in to at least that level. His next thought was he was going to have to move if he didn't want to get drenched with the next tide.

Screwing up his eyes in anticipation of the coming jackhammer rebellion in his head, he began crawling up the rocky, slippery incline to get above the tide line. By crawling on his elbows, wet, bedraggled and miserable, he made it to the upper level, and once there he turned to look around this new level of his dungeon.

Just visible through a door on the other side of his cell was a faintly lighted rock staircase. The dim light gave the steps an eerie, dull glow, for which Ari was grateful, as it wasn't bright enough to aggravate his headache. As he studied his surroundings, he heard the lock in a door above   the   staircase   turn   noisily.

5 S.O.S

Taman nervously fidgeted with his almost untouched beer. He had orders from the Raven to observe and not get involved in any ruckus. Figuring he'd be better off outside the Black Cat, he rose to leave, tossed some euros on the bar and walked out. Louie was busy with Jacques and Henri, so paid him no mind.

As soon as the door to the Black Cat closed behind him, Taman's demeanor changed. He quickened his leisurely pace. He looked all around him, checking his back trail, trying to see if anyone was following him. To a trained observer, he acted as if he had something to hide.

From Taman's position, the closest cover was the same fish market where Ari had hidden earlier. He walked into the shadows, pulling out his cell phone. As he entered, he wrinkled his nose, his senses rebelling at the overwhelming stink of aged fish.

He headed to one side of the market where he hoped he would be out of view. Once there, he poked his head around to look back toward the Black Cat, checking again to see that he was not followed. When he was certain he was unobserved, he pulled out his phone.

As a new customer at the Black Cat, Taman was not privy to the security arrangements; he was not an insider. As such, he was not aware Louie had the invisible Shorty covering his back. As Taman pulled out his cell phone, Shorty – squeezed into the priest's hole above the Black Cat entrance – paid him extra-special attention.

By now, Louie had finished his conversation with Jacques and Henri. He was back behind the bar drying glasses and still trying to figure out if his operation was in danger. He would hate to have to give up the Black Cat, but if his human trafficking business was under surveillance by the authorities, he would have no choice.

He shrugged his shoulders, acknowledging to himself, *C'est la vie*

(That's life). In retrospect, he realized it was not a good decision to use his family's waterfront bar to headquarter his business with the Bratva but he had needed the money, so...

His mind jerked back to the present when the bell rang again. He turned to pick up the speaking tube, putting it to his mouth, aggravated.

"What is it this time, Shorty?"

***

Inside the fish market, Taman nervously punched in some numbers on his phone, certain he was unobserved. Soon, a voice answered, betraying a certain level of anxiety. "Rafik, this is not a scheduled call, explain. Do you have an emergency?"

"Yes, sir."

"What is it?"

"That guy you warned us about, you know, showed us his picture? You said his code name was Raincoat..."

"What of it?"

"He was here, tonight, at the Black Cat..." Silence greeted Taman, and he grew anxious as the seconds ticked by.

"I see. Where is he now?"

"A pit under the Black Cat."

"Go back to the *Sahara*, get out of port, and maintain a position three or four miles off the coast. I'm sending Team 1. Nothing must interfere with your assignment to pick up the next container tomorrow."

"And when do I get my ship back?"

Stangl chortled light heartedly. "Getting tired of that old tub, are you?"

"The *Sea Wolfe* is in my blood, sir."

6 BOYS ARE STUPID

Inside the Black Cat Pit

Ari knew he was running out of time. The lock to the upstairs door screeched noisily, rebelling as it opened, pushed over an uneven rock floor. The rusty hinges had not been oiled for years, they too squeaked in pain. The salty atmosphere corroded everything metallic or wooden.

He had to think fast. His condition had not improved much. His head still throbbed, and even sitting up, motionless, he shivered. His bruised ribs added to his already nearly unbearable pain.

Ari knew he had no easy escape, but he searched the confines of his cell. It had two levels. The lower level where he had fallen had the locked grate, and that lock looked formidable, not a potential escape route, he decided. Three feet higher was the rock ledge where he now sat. And just above him was the iron door that led to the upper level and the Black Cat.

As the upstairs door opened, the faint light in the stairway grew slightly, shining down into Ari's cell. It was followed by the sound of heavy feet on the rock steps. Ari knew, in his present condition, he was not well enough to offer any resistance. He decided to feign unconsciousness, lying back down on the ground. From the outside, he heard Jacques lead Henri down the steps to the cell door, which was unlocked.

Both henchmen entered the pit and stopped after a few feet away, momentarily standing still to watch Ari. Unsure about him, they approached cautiously, still trying to ascertain his condition. It took every ounce of Ari's willpower to keep his eyes closed, knowing at any second they could launch an attack on him and he was defenseless.

"Jacques, give me a hand; there will be hell to pay if he drowns. There's going to be a high tide tonight."

They dragged Ari over to a higher spot in the pit, and Henri stopped to look him over suspiciously, not convinced Ari was unconscious. He inspected Ari closely and after a quick, brutish look at Jacques, Henri kicked Ari in the gut. He waited a few seconds, then launched another kick, waiting to see if there was a reaction.

It took all of Ari's self-discipline to control his response, exhaling with a painful grunt after each kick, he remained motionless. The kicks landed on Ari's already bruised ribs and the pain sent lightning strikes – almost like meteors on a moonless night – through his head. Ari secretly swore an oath that this Frenchman would pay.

"Search him," Henri ordered.

Jacques bent down to go thru Ari's pockets. He pulled out some money and a cell phone that was crushed by the fall. Ari could feel Jacques' hands going through his clothes. He continued to play dead and not make even a feeble attempt to retaliate. By now, they were both convinced Ari was out cold and had nothing more of value in his pockets. Satisfied, Jacques stood up and gave everything to Henri, who, with a typical French shrug of his shoulders, said, "That's all; he's out of danger from the water now, so let's come back later."

As Ari sensed their footsteps receding out the prison door, he chanced a peep from a slightly opened eye to see Henri and Jacques leaving the cell to return upstairs to the bar. Then he rolled into the fetal position, cradling his battered ribs, almost in tears and breathing heavily. He tried to concentrate on his situation – anything to take his focus off the pain.

He was puzzled; he had spoken to no one since arriving in Marseilles, so there couldn't have been a leak to alert Louie of his intent to question Taman. If there wasn't a leak and no one had sent an alert, it could only mean Louie and his men were up to no good and were much too nervous about any strangers who came in asking questions.

***

Upstairs, Louie stood behind the bar, tending to his customers,

Gauloise still hanging slovenly out of the side of his mouth. He noticed Jacques and Henri come back too quickly and signaled them with a nod of his head and a sideways movement, telling them to go to the empty side of the bar.

As they walked through the room, Louie matched their pace behind the bar, anxious to find out what they had learned.

"Eh, Alors?" *What happened?*

"He is still out from the fall."

"Still, huh?"

Jacques and Henri both nodded their heads simultaneously and Henri put Ari's possessions on the bar, eager to get rid of the stranger's few belongings. Louie looked them over, picking up the broken phone.

"Broken?" Both nodded.

"No ID, huh?" Louie pretended to look at the possessions in his hand, but in truth, he was again trying to plan his next move. He was running out of time and needed to know whether Ari knew anything. "I want you back in the morning; we will question him then."

***

In Ernest Hemingway's *The Sun Also Rises*, when asked "How did you go bankrupt?" Mike answers flippantly, "Two ways. Gradually, then suddenly." And so it is with the tide.

Generally, the tide in Marseilles take a little more than six hours to go from high to low. The level and timing depends on various planetary forces, primarily interaction between the earth, sun and moon. The water level gradually turns, then suddenly it has completed its reversal and is approaching high tide.

The sound of the early morning tide had been knocking on Ari's subconscious for some minutes. Still concussed from the previous day's fall, his mind refused to acknowledge the unwelcome interruption. It was only when the incoming tide interfered with his breathing that he was forced to acknowledge the intrusion.

It woke him, spitting and gagging at the unusual salty taste of the water in his mouth. He opened his eyes, making to sit up, only to be greeted by another rush of pain in his head. Still feeling much the worse for wear, he quickly closed his eyes, trying to mask the pain from his aching skull. He inched back away from the water and lay back down again, determined to take it easy.

As much as he tried to relax, his subconscious kept nagging at him. Something else was wrong. Ari had to pay attention; this same sixth sense that flashed warning signs at him had saved his hide many times.

Suddenly, Ari was completely alert, his eyes wide open, something gnawing at him, forcing him to come to attention. There was a faint sound of metal scraping against stone. He couldn't place the source of the noise.

He cocked his ear to the side listening, all thought of his bruised brains forgotten with the chant in his thoughts that something was out of place. Ari looked around the cell, searching intently for the source of the scraping.

In short order, he focused in like a laser on a spot where he thought the sound came from. He reached down to his foot to remove a shoe, and crawled noiselessly over to where he heard the sound. It stopped; Ari stopped, afraid he might scare it – whatever it was – away. He tapped his shoe, and was amazed to receive a tap in response, then two taps.

***

The Black Cat - Cell adjacent to Ari

In a cave, almost identical to the one in which Ari was imprisoned, the dungeon air reeked of the sea – not the sweet smell of a morning breeze arriving with the tide, but the polluted stench of man's intrusion on the oceans: saltwater, diesel and death, all mingled in an oppressive, humid trap.

A boy and a girl lay stretched out on the floor, head and arms facing the wall. Their hair was matted down on greasy foreheads, and they were scruffy, dirty and haggard-looking. Their shadowy eyes expressed a haunting sadness, a deep despondency, as if they had been exposed to cruelty or depravity no child should ever see.

Against the far wall were 25 other children of many different nationalities, all grubby and frightened, huddling together for warmth and support. Their eyes had the vacant look sometimes seen on the faces of concentration camp inmates. Silently, they watched their two unelected leaders decide what they should do.

Gareth, a young Welsh boy small for his age with curly dark hair, lay next to a cute, but opinionated caramel-skinned girl named Renee. They were clearly in charge and huddled close, whispering to each other.

Gareth appeared to be trying to convince Renee of something. "I tell you, my Da and I used to play this game; he said in an emergency I should tap dot-dot-dot, dash-dash-dash, dot-dot-dot."

Renee remained unconvinced, she looked down her nose at Gareth snootily. "My Mama used to tell me to be very careful of English boys, too, so there."

"I am not English, I'm Welsh, don't you French girls know anything?" Gareth responded indignantly.

"And I'm not French! I'm … I'm … Well, I'm from all over, and we lived in France, but—"

Gareth cut off her rambling explanation of her diverse family history. "And what difference does any of that make at a time like this?"

He received a withering stare for his trouble. "You boys are crazy.

What family plays a game where you practice like that for an emergency? Anyways I think boys are stupid."

While forming a suitable reply to Renee's challenging remark, Gareth's attention was diverted by a sound. "Did you hear a noise next door?"

He turned to look at Renee with an impudent, *I told you so* grin. "Not so stupid now, huhhh?"

They both put their ears to the wall, listening. Gareth resumed his systematic knocking, dot-dot-dot…

Ari's Cell

Ari had his ear to the wall, listening for the mysterious faint sounds. Above the tapping of Morse Code, he could swear he heard a little boy's voice, soft but still identifiable. "Not so stupid now, huhhhh?"

Ari recoiled in surprise, shocked to realize the voice was the sound of a child in what must be an adjoining cell. Faintly, he heard the voice of a little girl, speaking English with a slight accent. It may have been French or … It was hard to define. *Like my accent as a child,* Ari thought. *It changed with all our travels until it wasn't any nationality or culture, but just our family.*

"Boys, quelle peine (*what a bother)!* "

Ari choked back a laugh, still unable to believe what he heard, but captivated by the possibility that his sassy little niece was just inches away on the other side of the wall, he wanted to yell her name. As he started to shout out, "Renee!" he heard the sound of the key turning in the lock at the top of the stairs.

He kicked the wall between them as he sat back quickly, warning his young neighbors to be quiet. Then he moved away from the wall, just in time to hear the sound of his cell door opening. The increased light from above, as faint as it was, was still strong enough to partially blind his eyes. He closed them, but listened to the footsteps enter his cell.

Ari had to make a quick decision – attack or submit meekly to another bout of gut kicks from Louie's henchmen. Nearly twenty-four hours without food or water left him weak as a kitten. As the cell door swung closed behind Henri and Jacques, a large bright flashlight zeroed in on Ari, who could sense the light as bright redness against his closed eyelids.

Ari leaned back against the wall mere feet from where he had heard the tapping from the cell next to him. His muscles felt like rubber and his clothes weighed twice as much with the clinging moisture of the sea water that would not dry. As he heard Henri lumber toward him, he kept his eyes closed, sensing the distance of his mark. When he could feel Henri standing just above him, Ari kicked up suddenly with both feet, landing a solid blow to the rotund Frenchman's mid-section.

The unsuspecting lout had been leaning toward Ari slightly, thinking he had fainted again out of weakness. With the wind knocked out of him, he doubled over so that his face was mere inches from Ari's. Ari opened his eyes as Jacques dropped his flashlight, digging in his belt for a weapon. He looked up at Henri now, saw how close he was and hit him with the only weapon he had that he knew he could still wield – his own skull.

The blow nearly sent them both into unconsciousness, but as Ari grabbed at the wall, attempting to stand while Henri fell in front of him, he realized what weapon Jacques had been wrestling with – just before the Taser barbs pierced his chest and sent him sliding to the floor in spasms and pain. Before Ari could recover, Jacques had his hands bound and Henri was recovering enough to bind his feet.

Jacques sat Ari up to glare menacingly in his face. "Ze boss wants to know what you were doing at the Black Cat." His French accent was heavy and slow.

Ari had his back to the cell door. The two thugs faced him, and behind them was the locked grate to the sea, where the tide rose and fell gently.

Ari was in bad shape, shivering from the cold, still feeling the Taser effects and the headache from the fall, now doubled from the blow he had added during the fight. He closed his eyes, wincing. When he opened them a notch to look at his captors, his attention was drawn to a bright light coming from under the water beneath the grate, almost as if... Ari blinked, refocusing his eyes. Almost as if someone were using an underwater cutting torch.

Jacques looked at Ari, who immediately returned his gaze to his aggressors. They were determined to make Ari talk, and as if Ari needed more convincing about the seriousness of his predicament, Jacques began slapping his truncheon in his hand, approaching ever closer.

Ari realized it was not his imagination, someone or something was underneath the grate. He tried not to look so as not to give them away. He knew now he needed to play for time, as Jacques moved within striking distance.

"I work for Greenpeace," Ari said as he considered using legs and his last ounce of strength to sweep Jacques's feet out from under him. "We have some recovery work we want to talk to Taman about."

If Ari thought his subterfuge would work, he was sadly mistaken; all it earned him was a thunderous, teeth-jarring slap across his face.

"The boss told us to get the truth from you, no matter... It's up to you how difficult you make it for us."

Ari turned his head back from the recoil of the hit to his cheek, exercising his jaw to see if there was anything broken. As he returned his gaze to his attacker in front of him, he saw a silenced pistol emerge from the grate, followed by a hand. Just visible behind the hand was a snorkel mask. Before Ari could even look to his two inquisitors, the mysterious hand with the pistol fired two shots. Ari watched in some surprise as

Jacques and Henri slumped to the floor. Then he began to smile, feeling relief, despite not knowing who lurked beneath the grate.

Ari watched the hand with the gun move from targeting Henri and Jacques toward Ari. Weakened further by his beating, he stared down the barrel of the gun, unable to move and mesmerized as the gun fired. He did not even have the strength to flinch as he saw the muzzle flash.

Ari slumped to the floor, his eyes flittering closed. The shooter pushed up the grate and rose slowly into the cell, a ponytail dripping behind the dive mask. The diver, carrying a diver's bag, approached Henri and Jacques and bound them hand and foot, then turned to Ari.

As she was about to pull Ari toward the grate, his eyes fluttered open in a last conscious effort to put off sleep. He looked at his rescuer unmasked, and even in her wetsuit hood, he recognized her.

"Katarina," he said. Then more faintly, "Katarina, what are you doing here?" Delirium set in. "Why did you—?" The last was so faint the woman couldn't hear him.

She pulled Ari toward the grate by his shoulders, then placed a diving mask over his face and a miniature breathing aqualung, in his mouth. As he was pulled into the sea, the grate closed behind them. The shock of the cold water temporarily broke through Ari's unconsciousness, causing him to take a deep breath from his mouthpiece.

7 QUESTIONS TO ANSWER

Consciousness came slowly to Ari. His eyelids blinked uncontrollably, followed by an uneasy feeling of gentle movement; it was as if the floor underneath him swayed gently, backward and forward. Ari tried to gather his senses, eyes closed. Am I moving? he asked himself in his semi-conscious state; he wasn't sure. When he opened his eyes, he saw no light; then the reason for his discomfort became apparent.

In addition to his sense of movement, he heard the metallic noise of a can moving to and fro. The rolling sound was so rhythmic and consistent it reminded Ari of a metronome he used when he first took violin lessons.

Ari struggled to keep his eyes open, but it was as if he were still asleep. When he was sure his eyes were open, he still couldn't see anything; it was dark, pitch black. He tried to check his eyes, to see if he was blindfolded, but found his hands bound behind his back.

In the darkness, a gentle hand moved toward Ari's forehead cautiously seeking to dab his brow with a small piece of damp cloth. His eyes slowly grew accustomed to the dark, and he felt, or rather sensed, the hand on his forehead. A young child about 10 years old tried to comfort him. He strained to see, but could only hear the sound of many young children, crying, whimpering.

Struggling to see though the sparse light, he could just make out shadows, outlines – shapes of many small, scared children huddled in the far end away from him. His attention was diverted to the young girl trying to pull the gag out of his mouth. The floor under them started to swing more wildly, then clanged loudly as it hit a base underneath it. As the container they were in landed with a thud, there was a new movement – a gentle up and down as if a ship was getting under way, moving with the sea swells. Ari's compassionate savior finished removing the gag and dabbed his brow some more.

Ari whispered mystified, "Why are you helping me?"

"'Cause He sent you to rescue me."

"He?"

"I have been praying for you to come, I knew He would help me."

"How did I get here?"

"You were unconscious; they dropped you in." The little girl pointed up to a man-sized hole in the roof. "From up there…"

Moments later, the doors to the container swung open, and the oppressive heat was terminated by the ice-cold jet of a water canon aimed at Ari. He was knocked sideways to the floor, the small girl spread-eagled on her back.

LeFeu charged into the container, locked and loaded directly toward Ari; he didn't resist. She secured him from behind by his tied hands, and pushed him forward. Ari resisted the forward movement, turning around as much as he could to look at his captor. His eyes narrowed when he saw her ponytail.

She met his gaze, and nodded toward the children. "Let's take this outside."

Ari turned his head toward her, then responded indignantly, out of side of mouth. "You shot me."

"Not shot, tranquilized."

***

LeFeu's men led Ari directly to the Raven's private office, then hog-tied him to a chair, with LeFeu standing behind, ready for any resistance from him. He was totally confused. This soldier looks just like Katarina, at least I think she does. Self-doubt crept into Ari's thought process. She doesn't seem to even recognize me, perhaps I was mistaken.

Thoughts raced through Ari's mind at warp speed. If the Raven was the head of this child trafficking syndicate, could she be undercover? Might he blow her operation? She might still be with Athena, but from Moscow to here, that was a big jump. He decided to slow down, to only bring it up if they were alone again. Katarina's safety and the safety of the children came before any thought of his confused love life, or lack of it.

Before Ari had a chance to protest his treatment or even look into the mysterious woman's eyes, the Raven entered his office. Dressed in a blue blazer, grey slacks and a formal shirt opened at the neck with a cravat, he walked around to sit at his desk in front of Ari. The Raven noticed the hate-filled glare aimed in his direction.

"You probably want to kill me don't you?"

That's an understatement Ari thought. I'd love to throttle you, squeeze the life out of you, you perverted, sick monster. Instead of enunciating his true thoughts he said, "Predators who take advantage of precious, innocent children don't deserve to live." Ari's disgust and hate for Stangl was evident.

The Raven nodded, understanding. "I agree, Mr. Cohen." He turned his back on Ari to walk to the other side of the desk. The comment surprised and confused Ari. The Raven looked over at LeFeu as he picked up a sinister stiletto from his desk.

"Major, you may leave us; I will call you if I need you."

Somewhat surprised herself, LeFeu at first hesitated, then searched the Raven's face to make sure he was serious, receiving a slight nod from him, she left. The Raven walked around his desk to perch on the front, one leg supporting him on the floor, the other bent at the knee hanging lazily off the desk. He was so close, if I could only escape from the plastic shackle... The thought reverberated through Ari's mind. He was wary, watching the Raven closely, wishing he was the one with the stiletto in his hand.

Much to Ari's surprise, the Raven seemed relaxed, not angry, almost as if this were a normal social meeting. "You are an honorable man I believe, Mr. Cohen. I am going to release you from your restraints, if you will give me the time to make you a proposition."

"A proposition?" Ari's eyes rolled wide open. As much as he would like to exact his revenge, he found himself curious.
Stangl added, "Do I have your word?"

Ari nodded his agreement and watched dumbfounded as the Raven leaned forward to sever his bonds. As soon as Stangl was done, he started walking toward the door, looking at Ari.

"Come with me, please." He led Ari out of his room and down a corridor. After a few twists and turns, Ari and the Raven found themselves in front of a door with the sound of lots of happy children chattering within.

Dumbfounded again Ari asked, "What's in here?"

"The Sea Wolfe has a special dining room for the youngsters we recover."

"So you fatten them up before you take them to an auction?" Ari spat out.

"You will see, Mr. Cohen, just how mistaken you are." The Raven opened the door; inside were 20 or 30 children dressed in fresh clothes, eating ravenously and chatting happily. They were attended to by four kind-looking females, two dressed as nurses. The room was bathed in sunlight from the oversized windows reflecting another beautiful Mediterranean morning.

Ari was shocked and stood still, close to the door, leaning on the door jam. "But I don't understand, aren't you the ringleader of the child trafficking syndicate?"

Before Ari finished his question, the little girl from the container ran up to him and leaped toward him. Ari opened his arms wide to catch her, as he grabbed her, he stumbled back a little, surprised, then he steadied himself, as she snuggled up to him.

Ari was overcome with emotion. Looking teary-eyed at the girl, he asked, "What is your name?"

"Marie."

"Marie..." Ari sounded the name out to himself in a whisper.

Marie cackled out happily, "See I told you it would be all right. I prayed for Him to send me a savior and here you are... What is your name?"

"Ari…" He was completely taken aback, by her candor. "But, where are you from?" Marie suddenly tensed up, a sad frown overtaking her pretty face as she became defensive. She clung to Ari, whispering in his ear, "I don't want to talk about that."

Marie tried to change the subject, whilst still in his arms, she twisted around to point an arm toward the closest window. "Look, Ari, look, I've never seen the sea before." He followed her pointing arm, and looking out at the pristine waters, he squeezed her and hugged her some more.

The Raven watched the interaction with great delight. He tapped Marie on the shoulder. She looked over at him, the smile of childhood innocence.

"Marie, go and finish your lunch, Ari and I need to talk. He will come back later." Without a second thought Marie released her grip on Ari, but only after sneaking a last peck on Ari's cheek.

Ari watched Marie skip off happily toward the other children. He turned to look at Stangl. At the same time he couldn't help but ask himself, one question, Friend or foe?

Ari not only referred to himself but to the children. Had they been rescued by a ruthless mercenary who was only interested in profit, making money at the expense of these precious children of God, or was he a true angel of mercy?

The Raven turned to walk out of the dining area, "Ari, please follow me."

Stangl led Ari below decks, passing the crew areas that consisted of a crew mess, crew cabins and laundry. Even the crew quarters were sumptuous. They walked along a large corridor, and each room they passed had a shiny mahogany door with a polished brass plate, even the laundry room. Ari was impressed. He followed the Raven, who continued walking without even a glance backward to see if Ari contemplated some action against him.

8 THE TRUTH COMES OUT

Ari and the Raven walked back to his shipboard office. They were startled to hear O'Flynn's voice boom over the ship's comm system out of the blue.

"Mr. Stangl to the bridge please, *as soon as possible.*" His voice did not exude the confidence of a man in control or used to being in command of difficult situations; his tone higher than normal, and anxious.

Ari and Stangl immediately looked at one another, some unspoken thought passing between them. It was almost as if they were suddenly on the same team. They quickened their pace toward the gangway leading to the bridge.

Ari followed Stangl, who burst onto the bridge to see O'Flynn pacing. The captain looked up, relieved to see his boss. "Sir, we are under attack, radar indicates missile inbound from 50,000 feet."

***

The Black Cat, Marseilles

Henri, Jacques and Louie were in the saloon of the Black Cat sitting at a table away from the regulars. Smoke drifted lazily from their table as the three sat, leaning forward, deeply involved in a subdued, quiet conversation. Over at the bar, Shorty, the Priest's Hole watcher, acted as temporary barman to relieve his boss.

He tried his best to copy Louie's mannerisms. Gauloise cigarette hanging out of his mouth, wearing an undersized tank top, with a dish towel thrown nonchalantly over his shoulder, he wiped the bar top.

Louie was beside himself, angry as he'd ever been. "I should never 'ave trusted you two to do a simple job."

His face showed his fury, leaving Jacques and Henri terrified, cowering beside him and unable to offer any explanation. The two henchmen looked at each other, desperately seeking some answer, before looking blankly at Louie.

"Neither of you can explain what happened?" Louie almost screamed the words between clenched teeth, as he slammed his fist into the table in total frustration. Henri and Jacques jumped, but the blank stares remained.

Louie leaned forward conspiratorially toward his goons, then looked around the bar to make sure he was not overheard. "'Ow could you let that Americain take you both down?"

Gathering the courage to speak, Henri said, "But, Louie, *vraiment*, we were watching him, getting ready to interrogate him, and then we were unconscious. We don't know what happened."

Louie leaned even further forward as if he were about to share a great secret. "We can't take any chances; they might bring the law. We're going to have to move the merchandise."

***

As Ari and Stangl arrived on the bridge of the *Sea Wolfe*, LeFeu ran in from the other side. They all stood watching the electronic radar device tracking the inbound missile. As the projectile slammed into the sea, the thunderbolt of a terrifically powerful explosion rocked the *Sea Wolfe*. The missile had plunged into the water only 500 yards in front of them.

"I think someone is trying to get our attention, sir," LeFeu said in a rock-steady voice.

The Raven glanced at LeFeu, as if to say, *No kidding.* He turned to

O'Flynn, "Captain, reduce speed to one-third."

Ari observed all parties on the bridge. He tried his best to hide a big grin, but had his suspicions as to the missile origins. After all, if a missile had been fired *at* the *Sea Wolfe,* they would all be toast now.

He watched LeFeu, but saw no indication she recognized him.

Stangl seemed all too calm, as well. Assessing the situation, he said, "I agree, I think someone wants to talk to us."

O'Flynn, on the other hand, was in full panic mode, his eyes wide with fear, his complexion suddenly greasy. His voice betrayed his anxiety; in a much higher pitch he begged, "But, sir, we'll be sitting ducks..." His eyes were wide and terrified.

The Raven's contempt for his captain's terror was evident. Without even looking around to talk directly to O'Flynn he answered, "If whoever fired that missile wanted to hit us, we would already be dead. *Do as I ordered, Captain.*"

Ari watched the unusual dynamic – the Raven more in control of the situation than his captain, who appeared to be better suited to skippering an inland barge than an ocean-going, heavily armored, luxurious, yacht. The Raven was not only accustomed to command, which Ari would have expected, but he presented himself in an emergency situation as the Commanding Officer, assuming control as a matter of course.

O'Flynn was close to losing control, trembling as he reached to signal the engine room to reduce speed to one-third.

Ari tried to compute all that had happened in the last 15 minutes. He looked over at the Raven, still doubtful. The only thing of which he was sure was that Stangl had a dining room full of innocent children below that he must not endanger. He made his decision.

"If I may…" Ari walked over to the ship's communication console. "Is your satellite phone system working?" The radio officer nodded yes. "Get me 130-704-1776 stateside."

The tension on the bridge seemed to stretch out forever, everyone waiting in silence for either an explanation from Ari or for the phone call to be answered. A strong male voice replied, "This is Burke."

"Tom, this is Ari."

Burke's voice boomed back as if he were talking thru a loud speaker, "Ari, good of you to call."

"Tom, did you have anything to do with the missile that just landed 500 yards in front of the *Sea Wolfe*?"

Ari thought he heard a slight chuckle come over the line. "I thought your host might need to know you have a guardian angel watching over you."

"Roger that, sir, loud and clear. I think he got that message." Ari turned to look at the Raven as Burke's response came through the speaker. Stangl nodded his head almost imperceptibly, a slight crease appearing at the corner of his mouth. Then it was Ari's turn to add some levity, "Even the French Navy might have gotten that message, Tom."

"Is everything under control, Ari?"

"I'm not sure yet, sir. I think I need to have a talk with the Raven."

"Tell the Raven from me that he has two hours before I blast him to eternity."

"I think he knows you are serious, sir."

"Over and out, Ari."

No sooner had Ari disconnected the call than the ship's comm system crackled to life again. O'Flynn answered and listened before handing the device to his boss.

"Mr. Stangl, I have an emergency call from Captain Taman in Marseilles." The Raven turned to Ari and picked up the phone with one hand over the receiver, "Ari, this won't take a moment."

"Yes, Rafik, what is it?" Stangl listened without any verbal response. "Don't let them out of your sight, Rafik."

He turned to Ari. "Mr. Cohen, would you be so kind as to follow me to my command center?"

As he led Ari off the bridge, he said, "Mr. Cohen, I expect you are still wondering whether you should kill me or listen to me. Is that correct?"

He turned to look Ari in the eyes. Ari nodded, confirming exactly what was on his mind. "Mr. Cohen ..." The Raven opened the door to his private office, bidding Ari enter. "Please take a seat.

The two sat across from one another, and Ari finally said, "So, what do I call you?"

"Pieter will be fine; I am at your service," Stangl nodded his head slightly. "And may I call you Ari?"

As Ari nodded, the Raven began to explain. "I will not pretend I do not know you are aware of my ... past and certain connections I have acquired over the years."

"You mean the Sicilian Mafia out of Chicago? Yes, I'm aware you long held a position of great standing within their organization."

Stangl spread his hands before him in a gesture of acquiescence. "It was a ... family business," he said, unsure how much Ari knew. "After our ... experience with my brother, Wolfgang, I realized I could no longer be a part of that life. Getting out of the organization was difficult, and I paid a high price."

Ari had been part of the operation to take down Stangl's brother when he tried to sabotage the U.S. economy. Pieter Stangl had helped with that operation from behind the scenes and then had simply disappeared for months. When he resurfaced, it was on a report noting Stangl, a young Vietnamese boy he had adopted and his infant son had survived a vicious attack on his yacht when they returned to the U.S. His wife had not been so lucky. Ari knew a loss like that could drive a man back into the kind of world Stangl worked hard to escape.

"I see from your face you are acquainted with more of my story than I suspected," Stangl said.

Ari made as if to apologize, but Stangl cut him off. "It's fine, Ari. It simplifies things."

Stangl rose to pace the room as he continued. "I'm sure you can imagine what something like that can do to a man, and you would be absolutely correct. I went right back to the life I left, not because I wanted to be part of it again, but because I knew those connections would give me an opportunity to wipe away all traces of anyone who had anything to do with Jade's death.

"It was a lonely, obsessive mission that drove me night and day, and nearly cost me everything I had left," he said, turning back to face Ari.

"But as I prepared, again, to leave that life behind me, for the sake of my sons, I found I needed those connections even more." Stangl sat at his desk again and lifted a photo of his children – the young boy he had rescued, now a young man, and his own young child. He handed the photo to Ari.

"This is Theo and Lannie, my reasons for every breath," he said, pride painting each word. "Lannie is at a good university stateside. He is so smart and driven and has the most amazing heart." His voice softened and took on a tone of sadness. "Theo is down below. He is too tired today for visitors, but you may meet him later."

Ari handed back the photo and watched as Stangl set it back on his desk, handling it as if it were an item of immense value. "I knew about your trip to Vietnam, your wife and son and the boy you adopted. I'm sorry for your loss."

"Yes, Jade." Stangl smiled. "You would have liked her. She was very much like *your* Jade. So ironic that one led me to leave the U.S. so I could find the other …"

Ari gave him a questioning look.

"Madam President suggested I might best serve my country if I took shelter elsewhere for a while following the operation with Wolfgang. I think she hoped to spare me the suffering I had to undergo to leave the Cosa Nostra." He shrugged. "She did not understand the traditions that required sacrifice for freedom."

Ari nodded. There were painful traditions throughout his homeland in Israel and the surrounding nations.

"What's done is done," Stangl said, wiping his hands in a gesture of completion. "I took Jade home for burial, and then I left Vietnam with my sons and made my life about killing the men who ordered or condoned my wife's death. I lived for death," he rose again, anxious, and walked to the painting to calm himself, "until death came calling."

Stangl stood staring at the painting for a long moment, and Ari wondered what he got from the vision of such a sad time.

"My son was so young when they diagnosed him, and it changed everything for me," Stangl turned to Ari. "I left it all behind to be with the boys – Lannie was still homeschooled then. I suddenly understood what was important.

"But Theo just grew more and more ill. And then I saw a way to help him, but I would need those contacts – would need my old life.

"You see, Ari, with its diverse business affiliations, the Cosa Nostra is uniquely qualified to find and deal with these scumbags who prey on children, smuggling them throughout the world to fulfill the evil desires of human beasts. And whatever the mafia may be, my little world within it was family – and they protected children, not used them.

"So, when I needed children, it only made sense."

Ari's eyes narrowed again. "*Needed* children?"

"My son is dying. Without a donor – no, without THE donor – I will lose him. His doctor has developed a procedure that should cure Theo, but not without the right child ..."

"So you're kidnapping children to make them into human guinea pigs?" Venom dripped from Ari's words.

"In a manner of speaking," Stangl said.

Ari was on his feet and in Stangl's face with lightning speed. "You son of a—"

"Yes, I kidnap them from the kidnappers..."

Ari's mouth fell open and the hands he had rising to Stangl's throat fell by his side. "You what?"

"I take all of the children out of the child trafficking arena, feed and clothe them, and find them harbors of safety. If one of them is a match for my son, he or she will be used as a donor – a process completely safe for them.

"So far, we have had marked success," he looked pointedly at Ari, "but that was before you mucked about at the Black Cat." He smiled. "Still, it would be very helpful if we had someone from Athena, as well as Athena itself, on our team."

"So the children I came on board with, where did you get them?"

"They were already on their way here when you pulled your little stunt. The *Sahara* was in port waiting to make the exchange, and I sent in a team to add you to the shipment." Stangl smiled. "Not the deluxe accommodations I would have preferred for you ... or the children, but the operation works because we are thought to be part of it. No one knows that we remove the children from the pipeline."

"Because you funnel your efforts through the 'family business'?" Ari could not keep the contempt from his voice as he said the words.

"Precisely. All contact is made through the Cosa Nostra in Chicago – through my trusted people – working with the Russian Bratva. The children taken on board with you had already been offloaded from another ship and warehoused somewhere in Marseilles. We knew the Black Cat was involved, but did not know where he held the children before transport."

Ari was afraid to ask. "And the children who were in the cell next to me?"

Stangl started at the question. "Children? Monique had no time to sweep the area. She could not have known there were children in the cell next to you. Are you sure, Ari?"

"Yes. I heard them – a boy and a girl – I think it was my niece…" The words trailed off as Ari was overwhelmed by his grief. He looked up when he felt a strong hand on his shoulder.

"I came to rescue her," he said, tears in his eyes.

"And   we   will."

9 CALLING IN A FAVOR

The Athena Operations Center was tucked away in a quiet sector of Bethesda, Maryland, a far cry from its origins on the colonial estate of its founding leader, Thomas Jefferson. Burke eyed the man across the desk. He was not used to hearing Ari talk with this level of conviction and emotion.

"Ari, a decision of this nature is well above my pay grade. We would have to clear it with the Board of Directors." Burke could see Ari was adamant, almost like a python squeezing its prey until it succumbed.

"Tom, you remember you came to me in your hour of need when that Stealth bomber was shot down over Yugoslavia?" Burke knew what was coming; he should have predicted it. He sat back in his seat and tried to relax a notch and wait for it, thinking to himself, *Paybacks are hell.*

"Now I need your help, your resources. This isn't just about my niece; I'll find her if it's the last thing I do. It's even bigger than that. You know how many children are kidnapped and sold into sexual slavery worldwide every year, don't you? You read the report your team prepared."

"Yes," Burke replied, "I was thinking about that report the other day, it seemed rather detailed don't you think? As if somebody behind my back had my OPs team doing their homework. Strange wouldn't you say, Ari?"

Ari didn't flinch, instead he answered, "I'm told the hallmark of a good analyst team and field agent is to anticipate the questions of their Commanding Officer and to have that information ready."

Burke shook his head in resignation.

"Look, Tom, something has to be done, and we're the only ones with the resources to tackle this worldwide without the red tape tying our hands."

Burke just looked blankly at Ari. All he could think was, *Game, set and match to Ari Cohen; he's right.*

"Besides, wasn't it you who drilled into my head the moral responsibility we bear as members of Athena – carrying on the calling of the America founding fathers? What are those words again ... 'endowed by their creator with certain inalienable rights'? Freedom, Tom. Two hundred years ago, they created Athena to fight for freedom, not just for Americans but for the best ideals this nation has ever stood for."

Burke raised his hands in a sign of surrender. *He's right, this problem is too big to ignore, and if it's not an American problem now, it will be. We fought a civil war to banish slavery but it's alive and well all over the world and probably lurking in the underbelly of our own society. Something has to be done.*

This all splashed through Burke's mind, while he sat, hoping his face didn't show his thoughts or compassion. He knew Ari was right, but he wasn't going to let Ari know, at least not yet. "How many kids are sold into sexual slavery worldwide, Ari?"

"According to the report your team prepared, trafficking women and children for sexual exploitation is the fastest growing criminal enterprise in the world. Two million children or more are exploited every year in the global commercial sex trade. Almost 6 in 10 identified trafficking survivors were trafficked for sexual exploitation."

Ari paused for a breath, "Tom, are you telling me you would be willing to ignore those numbers, especially when we could do something about it?"

Burke sat for a moment studying Ari, who was unable to hide the righteous anger bubbling underneath the surface of his normally cool facade. He had to admire the fact that this man felt such a sense of decency to all these abused children, children he had never met. *Ari sees a great injustice and figures he can do something about it, and by golly he's going to do something about it – with or without us.*

Burke had only been waiting for Ari to take a breath, "Ari, I've already green-lighted an OP with the chairman."

"There is one other thing I haven't told you about, Tom." Burke didn't like the sound of that. He turned to glare at Ari suspiciously.

"And - what - would - that - be, Ari?"

"I want to bring someone in on this OP. We need him."

Burke returned to his seat, and examined Ari with great intensity.

"That is something only the board can approve, Ari. Who is it?"

"The Raven." Ari might just as well have gut-shot Burke, who stared at him as if he had lost his mind.

"Ari," Burke said shaking his head with uncertainty, "Are you talking about the same guy whose brother nearly bankrupted our country in the Swiss caper?"

Ari gave a simple nod of his head.

"But we don't have anyone who could vouch for him; that's a non-starter, Ari." Burke was in deep thought, "You know we have to have a board member of one of our founding states forward his name for consideration."

"Stangl thought you might say that, Tom; he suggested you ask Jade about him."

"You mean Jade McQueen, the President of these here United States of America? The same Athena Member from New York? Are we talking about that Jade?"

Ari almost felt like laughing; the reaction on Burke's face was priceless. He tried as hard as he could to keep his tone of voice as serious as possible, but after all the tension of the last few days, he needed a really good laugh. Instead he replied simply, "Yes, sir."

This was way too much for Burke, who sat looking seriously at Ari as he contemplated what the request meant.

"Do you mean to tell me you believe McQueen is going to vouch for the character of the Raven — one of the most serious criminal kingpins we have ever dealt with and a key player with the Cosa Nostra?"

"I know it sounds … implausible," Ari said with a smile, "but they apparently came to an … understanding during the Swiss operation. You know he contacted us through her and provided intel that helped put an end to his brother's plot."

"And then he went off and killed a whole herd of Cosa Nostra boys, Ari. That does not instill confidence in me for the content of his character, and I find it 'implausible' that he has become pals with the President of the United States!"

That did it. The rising crimson in Burke's neck and face and the climbing timbre of his voice undid Ari's resolve to remain professional.

He chuckled, which did nothing for Burke's mood, and then responded, "Yes, sir, he's fallen a bit off the straight and narrow, but you should really meet him, Tom. He has an excellent explanation."

Burke shuddered again. "I don't think I want to go through this twice; let's go down to talk to the member from Massachusetts."

Ari followed Burke down a long hallway past offices and workstations for the large operations center. He found himself wondering what the member from Massachusetts would think of his proposed operation and the new "asset" he wanted to bring in to Athena.

The hallways became a maze of turns, ending finally at a nondescript door. Burke pulled a simple key from his pocket to open it and they stepped through. Ari wondered whether they would have invited him through this door the first time if they knew the bombshell he would bring with him the second time he came down here.

"Watch your step." Burke reached to switch on an overhead light. The door opened to a set of stairs leading down into an undeveloped tunnel. After some time, the tunnel brought them to a set of old, wooden stairs and another unassuming wooden door. Another key came out of Burke's pocket, and he led Ari into what seemed to be the library of an old mansion.

The member from Massachusetts sat in a brown leather chair, reading a newspaper. He seemed not the least bit surprised when two men appeared from out of a doorway hidden in the bookshelves.

"Hello, Tom." He looked up from his paper with a warm smile and favored Ari with his glance. "I hear you have a new project for us to consider."

The big man chuckled at himself, rising to shake Ari's hand. "John," he said. "Have a seat. Good to see you again, Ari. We have a lot to talk about."

Burke quietly took up a position in the back of the room while Ari sat in the chair next to John. "Tell me, Mr. Cohen, what is this new crusade you would like Athena to help with?"

10 VIVE LA MORTE

Burke didn't like it, but then he didn't make the rules either. John, the member from Massachusetts, told him to perform a deep background check on the Raven. If things checked out, he would be working closely with Ari on operation *Forgotten*.

Ari had dreamt up the alias for the operation. He said he wanted to name it after all the neglected and abused children who would no longer be forgotten, at least not by him.

Surprisingly, there were only three alerts in Stangl's background check. The first red flag was in the form of the newly recruited captain of the *Sea Wolfe*. The second flag was his chief of security, Monique LeFeu. The third concerned the intercepted transmission from the Raven where he was buying 17 units of blood type AB.

"Stangl, I don't have to like the orders I am given, but as head of the Operation Center I do have to obey them." Burke waited for some reaction from the Raven, but the man was maddeningly calm.

Burke had decided to complete the interview process in an office Athena maintained on Wisconsin Avenue in downtown Bethesda for just such occasions. The highly secretive headquarters was only accessed by the chosen few with the highest security clearance. Athena needed a non-classified location to conduct business with people who had not been vetted, as well as to have a location for trade deliveries.

When Burke concluded Stangl was not going to open up the discussion, he didn't know a better way to proceed than to ask his question straight up, although he typically did not like to inform people that their communications were being monitored.

"We intercepted a call you made from the *Sea Wolfe* agreeing to buy 17 units of type AB?"

Stangl was quiet for a moment, the muscles in his face began to twitch almost as if the question had evoked a great emotional response from deep inside him, feelings that were still raw and painful. "I was wondering when you were going to bring that up."

"It appeared to us that you might be trafficking in children for organ harvesting purposes." Burke was expecting to see a denial, some form of surprise on Stangl's face. The answer he received surprised him even more.

"Of course it would," Stangl replied, "that is why we sent an unencrypted radio message that I hoped you would intercept."

This had been one of those days for Tom Burke, the kind of day where you wake up behind the eight ball and stay there. On a normal day, Burke thought he ran Athena from the OPs center, today he felt like Athena was running him. As if he had been away on vacation for three weeks to come back to a completely different reality.

Eventually he got a grip on himself, "We wondered why we were able to catch that message. Seemed out of character for your communications to be intercepted."

"This is going to be a long story, Colonel; you might as well get yourself a cup of coffee before I begin."

Burke eyed Stangl suspiciously. He didn't get up to refill his cup; he had that *behind the eight ball* feeling again.

As Burke watched the Raven, the man's demeanor changed. When Stangl first came into Burke's office, he strode in confidently, the walk of a Type A personality. The two men looked at each other now and it seemed Stangl was in deep emotional conflict, thinking of treasured memories his heart held dear. His posture no longer exhibited a ready-to-pounce, go get 'em readiness. He was transformed into a father, old beyond his years and weary from the world, telling old stories full of bittersweet memories.

Stangl looked up to face Burke; he was ready to answer the man's questions, one family man to another.

"Even Cosa Nostra bosses have families, Colonel. Two years ago, I found myself confronting such evil, that even I was shocked."

Burke was silent, letting the man in front of him tell his story in his own time.

The Raven looked up again and continued in a gentle voice, sadness radiating from every word, "Only my two boys remained. But my youngest, Theo, had a terminal illness, a type of cancer that could only be treated by a bone marrow treatment. Through my 'professional' contacts, I made inquiries to see if I could find a donor with matching genes on the black market. You see the official donor waiting list was so long that my son would not live long enough to benefit from official channels."

The Raven looked up at Burke as if pleading for understanding."I was willing to pay any price to save my son. Within two months, my inquiries resulted in three matches found in Africa. I paid the fee and waited for the matches to arrive. Ten days later, three boys showed up at my private clinic in an artificially-induced coma, ready to have their bone marrow and organs harvested."

Stangl looked up again at Burke as if telling this story was the most painful thing he had ever had to do. "You see these boys, on life support, were beyond resuscitation, their bodies, their lives, their hopes and dreams were over. All because I tried to save my son; it was all so unnecessary."

Burke shook his head gently, whispering, "Why?" His feeling of empathy for the Raven was uncharacteristic.

"The type of cancer my son had could not be treated by exchanging bone marrow with any donor, but only by arranging a blood transfusion from a genetic match who had the same 6 HLA (human leukocyte antigen) factors.

"To compound my guilt, these three donors died unnecessarily, Theo died before I could find a genetic match; we buried him at sea just days ago. I was hoping your satellites would pick up the burial service on the *Sea Wolfe*."

Burke didn't respond verbally, just shook his head sadly.

"To get back to the unencrypted message you picked up, your reputation at Athena is the best, Colonel, and I needed to get your attention. Even from within the Cosa Nostra, I cannot fight the Bratva and its web of helpful thugs on my own."

Stangl was greatly tormented, he sat in his chair, moving from side to side as if he wanted to get up to confront the evil he described.

"I'm sorry, Stangl. The Bratva has a long reach. I take it they have pulled in some help outside the 'family' to make up this trafficking network? Do you know who was responsible for the death of the three African donors?"

Stangl looked up at Burke, gone was the sorrow, replaced by a rock-hard determination to make sure his son had not died in vain.

"Yes, I do. He is number one on my list, a thug by the name of Tippu Tip; he runs his operation out of Stone Town, Zanzibar."

Burke cringed at the sudden hate, spewing from Stangl. *I would hate to be in that man's shoes when Stangl catches up with him.* It was as if Burke were looking at a different man. No longer the loving father telling a tale of his favorite son, instead a cold-blooded killer sat in front of him. *Ari and Stangl will make a great team; God help anyone who gets in their way.*

"Let's not waste time on things outside of our control, Colonel. I intend to honor Theo's memory by bringing MY justice to these immoral cretins who dare to harm and traffic in children."

Burke was clearly changing his mind about the Raven. "Theo, that's a good name."

"Theo Alessandro Stangl. He was named after his grandfather, who died in Vietnam. You might remember that from your dealings with my brother, Wolfgang."

"Yes, I do." Burke made his decision, but still had to verify two red flags. "Tell me about the captain of the *Sea Wolfe* and your chief of security."

Stangl sat back comfortably in his chair, smiling now that he was back on a less emotional subject. In a louder, confident tone he replied, "Don't worry about Captain Pedro O'Flynn, Colonel. I'm sure you are familiar with the expression, 'Keep your friends close, but keep your enemies closer'?"

Stangl watched as Burke, nodded in understanding, adding, "So his position in your employ... might be of a temporary nature?"

"O'Flynn is the missing link. He doesn't know it yet, but he is going to tell me all about his boss. He was the courier that brought those three comatose African boys to my clinic from Tippu Tip. It is his turn to *pay*."

Burke shivered, feeling the intensity of the Raven's hate for the syndicate monster who had committed this crime.

"Then," Stangl said, "I can get my full-time skipper back, Captain Rafik Taman. That's not his real name of course, and we buried his identity deep within his cover; that's why you couldn't trace him."

Burke thought he was beginning to get the picture, but couldn't help thinking to himself, *Crafty critter, this Raven, he might make a good acquisition for Athena afterall.*

Out loud he asked, "And Major Monique LeFeu? Her background seems rather difficult to check as well."

"It wouldn't be, Colonel, if you knew her real name. She used to be an Athena operative in Moscow, Katarina Azarov."

"WHAT? How the heck did she end up working for you?"

Stangl thought for a moment before responding. "Do you remember the Moscow affair some eight years ago, two Athena locals were assassinated in a restaurant in Moscow?"

"Yes, of course. Ari was there; apparently our people were innocent bystanders."

"Yes, but the Bratva confronted the local agents who helped Ari and exacted a terrible revenge. They also happened to be the syndicate in charge of child trafficking in Moscow. Katarina's sister was kidnapped; that's how we met. I'll get you her file, but I'd appreciate it if it was your eyes only. She didn't want Ari to know."

Burke nodded his head.

"This is going to be a long campaign, Colonel, but I am going to eradicate these criminal syndicates that traffic children, continent by continent," Stangl proclaimed with intensity.

"*We*," Burke said with equal ferociousness. "I'm going to recommend that one of our members have a chat with you to give our blessing and the final go-ahead."

***

Burke signed off on Stangl and his crew based on the Raven's word and the file he received on LaFeu… a file that did not tell her whole story, LaFeu kept secrets even from the Raven.

Algeria has long been the training ground of the French Foreign Legion. It was created by Louis Philippe, the King of France in 1831, its purpose to remove disruptive elements from society and put them to use fighting the enemies of France.

Even into the modern era, women remained barred from service in the Legion, the official version holding that only one exception was made – for a Briton named Susan Travers who first joined the Free French Forces during World War II.

The official version was wrong. Buried deep in the Legion archives was another file simply marked *Confidential, For the Director's Eyes Only*. This folder contained the personnel details of one recruit, Montaine LeFeu. What made the folder so sensitive was not the fact that Montaine was the only recruit to have assaulted a superior officer without receiving any form of punishment.

The fact that this recruit received no more than a hasty departure from the Legion was remarkable in itself, but not the main reason the file was buried. Hidden deep in the back of the file was the notation that the superior officer in question, Captain Vasily Borovski, had also resigned shortly thereafter amid rumors that LeFeu had not only beaten him in a fight, but had utterly subdued and then castrated the long-time Legionnaire.

It was the opinion of the officer's French commander that an officer in the Legion could no longer serve without the respect of the men he commanded, which he had undoubtedly lost along with his private parts.

To make matters much worse, after the arrest of this recruit, it was discovered Montaine LeFeu was in fact Monique LeFeu. The woman had followed Borovski over Europe by the depraved trail of ruined lives and the ruined futures of little children he left behind. One of the abused happened to be LeFeu's sister.

Borovski made only one mistake – he thought he could disappear in the French Foreign Legion, the reputed home of Europe's cut-throats, crooks and sundry fugitives from justice.

Of particular note in the file was the fact that Legionnaire First Class Montaine LeFeu was whistling the Foreign Legion's parade ground song as he – or she – left the barracks for the last time. The version was the early 1960's tune *Non, Je Ne Regrette Rien* (No, I Regret Nothing) by Edith Piaf, a song that has been a part of The Foreign Legion heritage for many decades.

***

Athena Board Room, Bethesda, Maryland
Later that same day

John, the member from Massachusetts waited until Pieter Stangl and Tom Burke were seated.

"Mr. Stangl, Tom Burke tells me you are remarkably well informed about our little 'club'... the Eyes of Athena?"

The Raven knew this was coming, but he couldn't see any way out of the dilemma. *How much does the guy know? What can I tell him without betraying the confidence that I swore to safeguard?*

The Raven wished he could have found a way to talk to McQueen, but she had been out of the country and unable to answer his messages to the private line she gave him. And now that she was President, even with all his vast resources, he had been unable to perforate the rock-solid cocoon around her.

At the time, and after much thought, he had realized the solution to his problem would be solved by a radio transmission that would put Athena, and hopefully Ari Cohen, back on his trail. His plan had nearly gone terribly wrong; he had not anticipated the missile fired by Athena. *That sure got my attention.* But it also went to prove another point; he made the correct decision, trying to ally himself with the organization.

"I have heard rumors over the years, a couple of my associates have been connected to Athena, but I don't know anything specific."

"Excellent. Good, good," the member from Massachusetts said, adding, "I'm so glad you decided not to lie to us, Pieter; we are not complete fools."

Now it was Stangl's turn to look totally surprised, raising an eyebrow. Hesitantly he asked, "What exactly do you mean?"

"You just walked through one of the most sophisticated intelligence operations centers in the world – far ahead of anything at the CIA, FBI, NSA or anything overseas. Did you perhaps think we didn't know about the help you gave Jade McQueen?"

Stangl chuckled to himself. "Forgive me, but it pays to be cautious in my line of work."

"Yes, well, now we both know where we stand. Let me tell you a little about the Eyes of Athena. As you know, we are a secret organization, founded by the fathers of this nation, that has been around for more than two centuries." Seeing only curiosity, he rose from his seat, and pacing the room, he went on.

"We are the brainchild of Thomas Jefferson, himself, who saw a need for a group to run outside the control of the government, politicians, even the President, to safeguard the true values, beliefs, safety and needs of the United States. May I call you Pieter?" he asked. Stangl nodded his head.

"Things have changed considerably in these last two hundred years, Pieter, and Athena has found it necessary to change as well. I understand that you want our help with a child trafficking network?"

"Yes, I do." Stangl said cautiously. Prior to this meeting he was expecting to be the one talking, trying to sell the Athena team on the benefits of joining forces so he could further his plans. Now, he was beginning to feel that perhaps Athena had its own agenda he was about to learn about.

"We have agents from all over, Mr. Stangl, all the best at what they do and loyal to the cause of freedom. I'm told you have the connections necessary to make this operation work, and I suspect you are as highly motivated in this matter as we are."

The Raven's stare turned hard.

John nodded. "That, I would say, makes us perfect partners."

Before Stangl could speak, the Eye from Massachusetts held his hand in front of him as if he had something to add. "There is one thing I wanted to mention, Pieter."

Stangl's smile dropped like a chunk of ice separating itself from a glacier, and a tidal wave of acid suddenly rippled all the way through his belly.
"What would that be?"

"As the head of the Cosa Nostra in Chicago, I believe you are probably familiar with the family code, once you are in, there is no out?"

Stangl did not respond at first, he nodded his head slightly, an uneasy but familiar feeling crawling up his spine. He paid a high price to leave the Cosa Nostra the first time...

"I assume you are inferring that once I join this organization, there will be no turning back, even after we eliminate this threat we are working on now. Is that correct?"

Finally the Eye from Massachusetts exhibited a real smile. "You know it is always so nice to negotiate with someone who understands our business so thoroughly. Great! We have lots of work to do."

For the first time since Stangl and the Eye from Massachusetts started the conversation, John looked over at Burke. He picked up a small glass of water, then looked back to Stangl. "Here's to us," he said as he raised his glass mouth-high.

"I assume your first mission will be to find the African connection?" the Eye asked haughtily. Stangl nodded.

"If you wouldn't mind adding that mercenary Louie from the Black Cat in Marseilles to your list of undesirables, I would take it as a personal favor. Might have something to do with Ari's niece, you see. We always look after our own, Mr. Stangl."

With that, John picked up his newspaper and opened it to an interior page, giving Burke and Stangl no more consideration. They both got up to leave. As Stangl walked toward the door, slightly numb, he thought to himself. *I'm never going to play chess with that guy.*

Back in the corridor, just as Burke closed the door, they heard the Eye's firm voice from within the board room. "Welcome aboard, Mr.

Stangl!"

11 EMPTY ACTIONS

January 10, 2014

ASSOCIATED PRESS, AMSTERDAM – Authorities say two Dutch men accused in the abuse of hundreds of boys and girls were found hanged and brutally mutilated in their cells Tuesday in the Penitentiaire Inrichtingen Amsterdam, a prison complex in the Netherlands city.

The two prisoners were accused of prostituting underage children through online chat rooms, where personal meetings were arranged. Victims of the scheme who have been identified are said to have come not only from the Netherlands, but the U.S., Belgium and Spain.

Prosecutor Eric Von Dycke reported that police continue to investigate the deaths. A postmortem indicated the victims had been castrated prior to death. According to an anonymous source within the department, police have no leads in the case, but suspect family members of the abused children may be responsible for the brutal slayings.

A string of child abuse cases have horrified the Netherlands in recent years, leaving understaffed police departments at a loss to protect their citizens.

***

The Black Cat, Marseilles

"Boss, did you read this morning's paper?" Henri chimed to Louie, pointing to an AP article. Henri handed the paper to Louie, who started reading the headline, as he did, his left hand slid down between his legs to subconsciously protect his manhood.

Louie put the paper down and was quiet for a moment. "Then it is not a coincidence anymore; first Vasily was castrated while trying to hide in the Legion, now our Dutch connections have been neutralized."

"Do you think it's the police, Boss?" Henri asked.

"Nah, someone is trying to send us a message, and it's not the police – a rival gang perhaps. I dunno."

***

Amsterdam

LeFeu was out of uniform. In fact she was dressed as a carefree tourist. She had intended to take the train directly to the airport; she was waiting on platform 14a of Amsterdam's Central Station for a local train to take her to Amsterdam's Schiphol airport when she had a change of heart.

She couldn't understand her feelings. She had expected to feel like a million dollars, a sense of total relief, ready for a celebration. Instead she felt distant, as if the target of her revenge was meaningless.

She had taken care of the brutes who abused her sister; she should feel great. Instead, after she had hanged them, she felt nothing. She thought back to the first prisoner she confronted, sleeping peacefully in his solitary confinement cell. She had carried out her revenge with surgical precision. Her victim kept trying to scream through his gag, watching horrified as he lost his manhood. She knew what he was trying to say, but she didn't care. There was nothing he could offer her, no bribe big enough.

The second victim was even less remarkable; it just didn't matter to her. She had condemned them and was simply the executioner with a job to do. Nothing they said could bring her sister back.

LeFeu left the main entrance of Central Station with all her possessions on her back. She walked across Prins Hendrikkade to take a water taxi. It was late afternoon, and she walked down the concrete embankment to wait on the next ferry. After boarding, she had the front of the barge almost to herself, the one distraction, a middle-aged captain with a scruffy ponytail who smoked incessantly. The only time he wasn't smoking was when he occasionally talked on the radio or maneuvered to make the required, frequent stops.

Le Feu needed time to think. As the ferry departed, she tried to look out the plexiglass window, to act like other tourists. As much as she tried to enjoy the view of the historic buildings and the tea houses they passed, she couldn't; she couldn't see that far. Her eyes seemed to gloss over and all that appeared in front of her was her reflection in the window, her battle-saddened face. *Who am I? Am I this new assumed identity, am I Monique LeFeu? Or am I still Katarina Azarov? Will I ever be able to just be Katarina Azarov again?*

Thinking of her life in Moscow brought back memories of meeting Ari – the electricity she had felt the first time he put his hand on her lower back to guide her gently through a door. It was as if he had felt that jolt too because he withdrew his hand again unnaturally quickly.

Then she had seen him again. She thought back to her mission to rescue the prisoner in the pit at the Black Cat in Marseilles, remembered her reaction. She had tranquilized Louie's two thugs; now she realized she should have killed them, at least castrated them, but she had orders. She saw Ari after she shot Henri and Jacques. Even in his bedraggled state, she recognized him and that same bolt of excitement charged through her again. Surely it couldn't be him, here in Marseilles of all places.

He opened his eyes; it looked like he had to struggle to pull his eyelids apart, and after what seemed like a momentous effort, he squinted, not believing what he thought he saw. But... *No it couldn't be. How could he have recognized me? It was impossible, but, but it sounded like he whispered, "Katarina, Katarina, what are you doing here?"*

LeFeu stared at her reflection in the barge window, thinking to herself, *I must have been dreaming. But it did sound like he said just that...* She wasn't the type to get weak-kneed and misty-eyed over a man. She had always been pursued by men – beautiful, confident and sexy.

But seeing Ari again after she had pushed away all other lovers in her quest for vengeance … Her heart betrayed her aloof assuredness.

If I get on that train to the airport, take the plane back to Moscow, I might never see him again. She thought back to the reason she came to Amsterdam; the men who had kidnapped and abused her sister would not be mistreating any more children. Still, she felt deflated; she found Borovski's two accomplices, but the revenge she had prayed for had left her empty.

She had watched their eyes as she performed her revenge. At first, when she unfastened their pants, they looked expectantly at her, as if they couldn't believe their luck. But when she reached behind her to pull a scalpel-sharp stiletto knife from its scabbard, that was when the struggle and the panic started. They watched, unable to do anything as their organs were removed. They tried to squirm. They looked at her with pleading, questioning eyes. She didn't even give them the satisfaction of answering their unspoken question, *Why?*

With a surgical precision she had performed her cuts, but now that her mission was completed, she felt empty. After what happened to her sister, Elena, she left Athena a broken woman. It had taken weeks for her to come out of her down-trodden state enough to shift her guilt from wanting to die to needing to live for revenge. Elena was left broken because of Katarina, because of her ties to Athena, the only thing Katarina could do was to exact justice on those responsible for her pain.

She had spent several more weeks perfecting her cover story – with help from a friend at Athena who created a deep cover for her that would protect her even within the darkest corners of the criminal underworld. Monique LeFeu had been born, with the French accent perfected to cover Katarina's own purring Russian inflection. Monique LeFeu had tracked down Borovski, became Montaine LeFeu, so she could get close to him and joined the Foreign Legion.

Was revenge the only reason I joined the Legion? To maim that monster? Make him suffer? Katarina had lost her sense of purpose with her Athena ties – and the onslaught of guilt over Elena. Unlike most of the men who came to the Legion out of a life of crime, LeFeu had found purpose there – a purpose that had carried on in her work with the Raven. *If I get on that train, if I go back to Moscow, I go back to a "normal" life… what will be my purpose then?*

LeFeu stared long and hard at the faint image of her face in the window. *Perhaps I have found my calling. To do something for all these children… perhaps if I neutralize enough of these monsters, I will make a difference, perhaps, perhaps…*

LeFeu watched in surprise as a smile began to spread on the face staring back at her. *And so I will, I will be a crusader for the Forgotten.*

That was Ari's term for them – the children lost to human trafficking. In that moment, LeFeu made up her mind; she would go back to Marseilles to join the Raven and Ari in their quest.

And for just a moment, she allowed herself one other thought… *Perhaps, just perhaps, Ari did recognize me, and perhaps he felt that attraction, too.* Time would tell. But there were more important issues at hand, a certain ship's captain at the center of this trail of trafficked children.

She knew the Raven had kept him close because he was a member of Tippu Tip's gang. *I should start with him,* she thought. *I wonder how he will scream when he sees me coming toward his manhood with a knife in my hand. I wonder…*

12 BACK TO THE BLACK CAT

The Raven sat in the front of the Zodiac performing an equipment check on his FN FAL. After reloading the magazine with 30 7.62×51 shells and re-attaching the night-vision scope, he turned to aim the gun toward land, checking the scope settings. As he turned around with his back to the bow, Ari watched him intently.

Shouting above the engine noise as they plowed over the waves toward shore, Ari said, "Looks like you know your way around that FN."

Ari had seen a change in his host. Gone was the sophisticated billionaire in a sports coat; instead he saw a face he recognized only too well – that of a warrior about to enter battle. He had seen that same determined look in the mirror many times.

"If I'm going to cover your back at the Black Cat, you'd better hope I do," Stangl responded. He thought back to his early days in the Sicilian Mafia, where he had been respected for his education and ability to lead his men away from violence. However, that had not kept his "father" from ensuring he was trained well for any eventuality.

His brains had earned him a position as his boss's right-hand man before he left the Cosa Nostra the first time. When he went back to get revenge on everyone who had been involved in his wife's murder, his cold-hearted string of mayhem had left him with an unchallenged leadership position in Chicago.

Stangl smiled, seeing Ari's reaction. *Put a well-tailored blazer on a guy, buy him a fancy yacht, and everyone assumes he doesn't know which end of a gun to point. If only they knew.*

Ari and Stangl left the *Sea Wolfe* in the early hours for the three-mile trip back to the Port of Marseilles. As they approached within a half-mile of the lighthouse marking the outer sea wall, they slowed to a crawl. The engine now chugged quietly, so silently the eerie foghorn from the lighthouse bristled the hairs on the back of their necks.

In front of them, Ari could see the jetty leading to the fish market and, to the west, the Black Cat. He made a wide circle around to the far side of the fish market to drop Stangl off. He had re-checked his equipment and stowed it in a dark green duffle bag. As Ari pulled alongside the pier, Stangl pushed his bag up on the wooden dock, grabbed the ladder, and launched himself up with ease. By the time he had retrieved his bag and turned around, Ari had turned the boat and disappeared out of sight.

Within two minutes, Ari had floated under the pier leading to the pit under the Black Cat, secured the inflatable, and was waiting for Stangl's go-ahead.

Stangl watched the Black Cat from the fish market across the way, infrared binoculars helping him scan the building. He waited for the bar to close, and now the only hot spot still showing human life was in the Priest's Hole, one unmoving body, probably sleeping.

The Raven pressed the mic button on his comm system, "Ari, all quiet. Go."

"Roger, Stangl. Wish me luck."

Scuba diving in a busy freight and fishing port is only for the courageous. Fishing boats discard unwanted fish entrails and commercial freighters release fuel residues; and all of that waste seems to congregate on a diver's breathing mouthpiece. The more a diver moves his lips to rid them of pollution, the more it accumulates on the rubber mouthpiece.

Not looking forward to the next step, Ari nodded to himself, stealing his courage, then he slipped silently over the side of his inflatable and eased into the water. Before he was waist deep, he felt something bump his calf. Trying not to move, he prayed, closing his eyes, frozen in surprise, with his legs in the water and his upper body suspended on the side of his skiff.

He was motionless, holding his breath, secretly hoping the next surprise would not be the bite of an underwater scavenger. Ari counted the seconds, each millisecond seeming an eternity. Thirty seconds later, he continued into the water. Once fully submerged, he closed his eyes, trying to sense any movement close by.

Feeling a little relief nothing tried to take a bite out of him, he next turned to his breathing. He was sucking oxygen from his breathing apparatus as if he had an infinite supply. He tried to control his intake. The only sound he could discern was that of waves rocking against the dock. Feeling truly alone and not wanting to risk a light, Ari swam under the pier, feeling his way, moving ever so slowly until he arrived at the underwater hatch that opened to his previous accommodations, the pit under the Black Cat.

He checked his watch; only another 20 minutes to low tide. He would have to hurry. *If I can get to where they held me prisoner, make my way to the neighboring cell and find who was tapping Morse code, maybe I can rescue them, bring them out under the pier at low tide. They wouldn't even have to swim, just paddle or walk under the jetty to the meeting point with the boat, pick up Stangl and get back to the Sea Wolfe.*

Ari arrived at the hatch, pulled out his underwater hydrogen torch and cut through the lock that replaced the one Monique had ruined. He gently lifted the grate as quietly as he could. Every time the metal grated, he cringed, expecting to be surprised by someone from inside. The grate was so heavy, he struggled to maintain his grip and not let it crash to the floor. After a major effort, he laid the hatch down inside the cell. Now that he was free to look around, the light from the outside corridor cast a faint glow, enough to see his old cell was empty and the door at the front was open.

Ari pulled his communication gear from a waterproof bag and attached the headset.

"Stangl, all clear?" he whispered.

"All clear." As Ari listened to the response, he edged around the door to look down the corridor. Peeking around the corner, he noticed a camera perched high at the end of the hall, a faint red light blinked to indicate it was "live." Ari retreated back to his former cell and tapped his comm mic.

"Stangl, they have a live camera over the door; I'm going to neutralize it. When I do, it will set off the alarm, and reinforcements are going to arrive. I need you to take them out."

"Roger, Ari." The more time Ari spent around the Raven, the more he liked him. Stangl sounded competent. *I just pray he's a good shot.*

Ari closed his eyes, then charged out of his cell. The area outside was recessed, a slight safe haven where he could hug the wall before exposing himself in the hallway that led to where he hoped to find his niece.

His plan was simple. There was no point in trying to hide his approach. If the camera feed was monitored, the alarm would be given as soon as he was seen. The best he could hope for was to neutralize the camera before they could identify him.

Ari took a deep breath, peeked around the edge of his recessed alcove, took aim and shot out the camera. Before he even felt the recoil of his Glock, he was advancing into the corridor leading to the cell door. It seemed to Ari this entire area was chiseled out of rock or some form of limestone. It was as if he was in a cave – damp and cold. Even so, sweat pooled beneath Ari's diver's suit.

He took two steps before the ping of a bullet ricocheting off the wall next to his head got his attention. Standing in the corridor between him and the cell door he needed to access was the lumbering Frenchman, Henri. Both eyes were still showing the bruises from Ari's head but, fading, but still a deep purple. The look on Henri's face told Ari he was determined to inflict his revenge ten-fold on the man in front of him.

Ari ducked back into the recess to consider his choices. Retreat was no option if there was any possibility Renee waited in the cell just feet away. Henri was an obstacle that had to disappear.

Ari had only seconds before he reckoned Henri would venture around the corner. Ari rocked his head slowly side to side, loosening his muscles for the task ahead. He had dropped his tank next to the grate and removed as much of his suit as possible, but his dive belt remained and he slid the 8-inch, surgical steel blade from its scabbard. As it gleamed in the dim light, he lowered his head slightly, said a silent prayer that he was healed enough to get the job done, and charged around the corner to attack the man before him.

As Henri saw Ari leap from the recess, he let loose a guttural war cry and pitched himself headlong into the fray. He sidestepped Ari's first swing with the knife, seeing the blade just in time to avoid its razor-sharp edge.

As Ari spun past Henri, the thug grabbed his dive belt and pulled, bringing Ari to the ground with a sudden, bone-jarring movement. Ari lay dazed a fraction of a second before he felt the weight of Henri's boot on his neck. Henri thought the battle was over, but he had underestimated his opponent.

"Stupid, Americain. Why would you come back to die in zee pit?"

Ari could not have replied if he wanted to, instead he drove the knife deep into Henri's ankle, thankful the man had not been smart enough to disarm his opponent. Henri wailed in pain and rage, falling backward into the wall of the corridor.

Alive with adrenaline, Ari was up and at Henri's throat so quickly the man didn't have time to blink. Ari stared into the man's hate-filled eyes, his fetid breath enough to nauseate Ari. "Where are they?"

Henri glared back at Ari, but made no sound. Ari increased the pressure on the brute's throat and added the cool steel of the knife blade for good measure. "Where are the children?"

Henri's eyes looked toward the cell where they had been kept. Whether they were still there or not, Ari doubted the dolt would know, probably not being being privy to Louie's secrets. He spun the knife in his hand and dealt a withering blow to the back of Henri's head with the heavy handle.

Then Ari placed a charge with a two-second timer on the cell door lock and moved on to hug the far wall, outside the blast zone.

He waited for the charge to blow. The percussion from the explosion vibrating his eardrums and causing a quick, teeth-grinding spout of pain. He had wasted too much time with Henri and knew others would be coming soon if they weren't already on their way.

He moved back to the cell through the smoky residue of the explosion and kicked open the door to charge inside. He entered quickly, leveling his Glock in front of him and searching carefully along the barrel of his gun for any sign of the enemy... or of the children he wanted so desperately to find.

The explosion on the door caused the low-wattage light bulb to swing wildly above his head. His sixth sense told him he was too late, that he was alone, but still he searched. His eyes followed the path of the arcing light of the swinging bulb.

The light swung toward the wall separating this cell from the one where he had been held captive. His gaze followed the light, and he stopped breathing; he couldn't be sure, but he thought he saw a drawing on the wall that he recognized. Renee, as a child, had adored drawing. Her favorite subject, mermaids. But, Ari thought to himself, I must be losing it. A moment of doubt crept in, and before he could be sure, the light was gone, swinging toward the other side of the cell.

The light swung ever so slowly; he paid scant attention as it swung away from his area of interest. As the light swung away, he forcefully tore his eyes from the drawing on the wall that had shocked him. Now his subconscious mind was trying to telegraph to his conscious shocked brain, *Warning! Warning! Danger!*

Ari's adrenaline surged and his thought process was overpowered with the possibility he had been this close. By now, his subconscious hammered his brain like a jackhammer, screaming at him to wake up, pay attention. His training re-asserted itself and he pulled his eyes away from the wall he wanted to inspect further.

Everything moved in slow motion. His training told him to look to the right, his heart told him to wait for the light to shine on the left wall. What got his attention was a blinking red light attached to a small package hidden in a recess of the back wall.

His subconscious had been right; his eyes had seen it and, honed by years in the field, had recognized the danger. But his conscious brain was under the control of his heart. He had known all along there were two wires circling the package around the blinking light.

Just as he recognized the light, he heard a voice from the corridor behind him. "Foolish Americain! There is no place for you to escape!" Footsteps running in the opposite direction told him all he needed to know about the length of time until detonation. He dove for the open doorway...

***

No sooner had Ari warned Stangl of the expected arrival of reinforcements than the shape in the Priest's Hole jumped up, alerted somehow. Stangl followed Shorty's movements through the infrared scope until Shorty seemed to sit still. Stangl squeezed the trigger, aiming for the deepest red signal that indicated the sensor's hottest reading. The image jumped, as if in total surprise, then seemed to slump back to the floor.

Sounds from the street outside the Black Cat told Stangl he was in trouble. Satisfied the lookout in the Priest's Hole posed no further threat, his attention was drawn to a men charging toward the Black Cat entrance. Stangl moved his scope to line up on the door.

Jacques and Louie stopped at the door to unlock it. Their delay to get in the door gave Stangl the perfect shot. He fired once, and as the man at the back slumped to the ground, he fired again – a total of two shots, almost simultaneously.

Stangl watched through his scope as the hunks of meat in front of the

Black Cat door moved no more. He grinned to himself, *I haven't lost the touch,* and began to relax.

He tapped the mic on his comm gear to let Ari know all was clear, but before he could utter a word, the whoompf of a significant underground explosion knocked him out of his complacency.

Stangl switched the channel on his comm gear and shouted down the mic, "Monique, get in there; Ari's in trouble."

13 SHARED SECRETS

Ari floated in some distant place. It was as if his soul were disconnected from his body. Ever so slowly, sounds penetrated his being – voices, a man and a woman whispering close to him. He was pulled back from that place where his mind floated, back to a body racked with pain. He didn't want to go back; he was so comfortable floating, pain free.

Slowly, he became aware he was back in his body. One by one, his senses returned to him. At first, he felt pain in his chest, and the very act of breathing was a struggle. Then he heard the sounds again and struggled to concentrate, to listen to the words, but he was floating in a fog bank.

The bright lights above discouraged any effort to pry open his eyelids. Some words penetrated his subconscious, but it took too much effort. He tried to move his hand to shelter his eyes from the light; his arm was secured. He felt an intense stab of pain at the back of his hand. Everything hurt too much. *Go away pain,* were Ari's last thoughts before he returned to his deep slumber.

"He has a severe concussion." Dr. Drakul said gently, standing to one side of Ari's bed as he finished inserting the IV into Ari's hand. He whispered to LeFeu, "It will interfere with the normal functioning of his brain."

LeFeu turned away from Dr. Drakul to his patient in the bed of the intensive care unit of the *Sea Wolfe*.

"It may affect his memory, his judgment and perhaps speech. We must be patient." She heard the doctor's words, but wouldn't take her eyes off Ari's face.

She rubbed the back of her hand over his forehead. "Isn't there something I can do to help him, doctor?" She tenderly stroked Ari's brow.

"Keep talking to him soothingly, gently. You might find he is unable to remember things when he awakes. He might ask the same question repeatedly, not remembering having already asked it. He might complain of headaches, dizziness and the need to vomit. Sometimes there are coordination and balance problems, and blurred vision or ringing in the ears are also common symptoms."

Their quiet contemplation of Ari's condition was interrupted by the door swinging open noisily, banging on a doorstop as Marie flew across the ward floor, pleading loudly, "Is he going to be all right?"

Concern and fear were evident in her voice, but she managed to slow down a bit before she launched herself gently on top of Ari, burying her face in the pillow next to his face.

Dr. Drakul hurried to the side of the bed, imploring the child, "Marie, please be—" He stopped in mid-sentence, surprise spreading across his face into the widest of smiles. Ari's left hand, the one without an IV connection, lifted up slowly toward Marie's head. At the same time, he inched his face around, allowing him to bury his nose in her hair.

Dr. Drakul and LeFeu remained motionless, eyes widening as the patient and his visitor snuggled and hugged one another. All was silent in the ward as two lonely humans took comfort in each other's love. It seemed as if time stood still, but the hand caressing Marie began to move slower with each passing second. As if the effort were too much for Ari, the hand slipped back down, reacting to gravity, gently returning to its berth alongside Ari on the bed. His muscles relaxed as he returned to his comatose-like state.

For a moment or two, no one said anything; the three simply looked from one to the other, before Marie chimed out arrogantly, as if the Doctor and LeFeu could not possibly know more than she did,

"See, he's going to be fine." Then she added thoughtfully, "You know I prayed for this; I told God I needed a new Papa!"

***

The *Sea Wolfe* Library

Marie had never seen such luxury before. She breathed in deeply, enjoying the smell of aged leather. She turned to look around the spacious library, Stangl's private reading room on the *Sea Wolfe*. LeFeu sat beside Marie, examining her new ward with pity on her face. She felt a deep pain for any child who had suffered at the hands of the trafficking trade. She hated to think of the atrocities this child must have endured.

Marie turned to look at the straight-back chair she was sitting in. She lifted her hand to touch the elevated rim at the back, trying to guess what it had been made from, but she was puzzled.

"What is this?" she asked, stroking the surface that extended from her armrest to form the back frame.

"It's a Kudu horn," Monique replied.

"Kudu?" Marie sounded out the word as if it's very pronunciation was a secret.

"A big African antelope, very special."

Marie continued to look around the library, her eyes taking in the opulence, but another puzzled look crossed her face.

"Are you sure I'm allowed in here?" she asked suspiciously.

LeFeu smiled, enjoying the child's natural curiosity, but she knew it was time to get serious. Ari showed all the signs that he was going to recover. When he remembered he was unable to find his niece in the bar in Marseilles, he would fret, wanting to follow the trail as soon as he was able.

She reached over gently to Marie, trying to comfort her by stroking her hair, as if she were brushing Marie's locks with her bare hand.

"Marie," Monique started gently. "We need information; I brought you in here because we need your help." Marie's countenance changed immediately; she turned, attentive, but cautious, lavish surroundings forgotten immediately.

"Where are you from, Marie?" The girl tensed again. She was back on guard, distrusting. Monique sat silently, waiting patiently for her to answer.

After a long pause, she responded in the faintest of voices. "I'm from Paris."

Monique nodded her head thoughtfully, thankful for the small break in Marie's distrust. After a moment of silence, Monique continued, "We are going to have to talk to your mother and father, you know, tell them that you are safe."

Instantly Marie's face hardened again. She became agitated, fidgeting excessively, looking away from Monique and pretending to be absorbed in an oil painting hanging on the wall.

Part of Monique's training with Athena included hostage negotiation. She knew Marie was trying to avoid this conversation and was not genuinely interested in the painting she admired.

After spending some time looking at the painting, Marie turned her puzzled look toward the plaque underneath it. She mouthed out the strange words slowly, "Auvers sur Oise by Cezanne." Trying to continue the subterfuge, she looked to Monique. "Is Cezanne famous?" she asked.

Monique knew the child was doing her best to change the subject, but decided to play along. "He was a very famous painter. Have you ever been to Auvers sur Oise?" she asked.

"That's a very funny question." Marie answered genuinely surprised, she was frowning childishly now. "Why would I ever go *there*?" she asked theatrically.

"Well, because it's on the outskirts of Paris; it's a famous community of artists. Lots of parents that live in Paris take their families there for a weekend outing."

Before Marie even realized she had been drawn into a conversation to open up about her life, she responded, "Oh, no, my Papa could never afford to take us there."

LeFeu seized the opportunity, "So you do have a father, then?"

Marie was back on guard, cagily answering, "Well, I don't have a father *anymore*." She paused to think, and again Monique didn't interrupt. After finishing her thought, Marie continued, "Well, I *didn't* have a father, until very recently," she added with a big smile.

"But I do now, you see, Ari is going to be my new Papa." Marie looked so trusting, her eyes those of childhood innocence, that Monique couldn't rebuff her statement. She leaned forward, resting her elbows on her knees, reaching for Marie's hands.

"What happened, my little darling? Tell Monique."

Marie's eyes began to tear up, her face flooded with emotion. The sudden release of grief tried to tug her lips apart, but she held on, keeping her jaws clenched together.

"You see my Papa had to sell me to the bad men." Marie couldn't restrain her torment any longer; she pulled her hands out of Monique's tender embracing fingers. She covered her face with her hands, but even that was not enough to hold back the torrent of tears flooding to the surface. Her little body shuddered with sadness.

"But I don't understand!" she shouted loudly as Monique moved over to the side of Marie's chair to hold her sobbing body.

"Why did Papa have to sell me to those terrible men?" She added in a shamed whisper, "They wanted to do bad things to me, you know."

Monique held Marie tight, waiting for her body to stop shaking with grief.

"Don't you see?" Marie asked through her sobs, "I can't go back; those men will kill me."

"What happened, Marie?" Monique whispered in Marie's ear. "You need to tell someone; you will feel better."

"Oh, I can't tell you it is too awful, what those men did."

"Tell me."

"We lived in a small apartment above a bakery. My Papa told me the whole street was owned by a gang of very bad men from Romania. If my Papa was late with the rent or couldn't pay on time, these men would hurt him or take my Mama away for a few days. When she came back, she would be covered in bruises."

"One day, that horrible man came by to collect the rent, but my brother had been sick, so we had to buy medicine for him. When he found out my Papa didn't have the rent, he was furious.

"The man looked around the room, and his eyes settled on me. He stared at me, wouldn't take his eyes off of me. Then he came up to me; he was so close I could smell his stinky breath, and he said. 'I'll take her,' pointing at me. My Mama screamed at him, so loudly, 'No! Take me; I'll do anything!"

Marie lay across Monique's lap now, her face turned away from her as Marie's eyes glazed over in memory. Monique's heart was pounding in her chest, the pain of Marie's story almost too much for her.

Marie took a long shuddering breath. "The man wouldn't take his eyes off me. He threw my mother aside, reached out to grab my arm and started pulling me. He took me from my family; he pulled me by my hair. Papa tried to tell him no, but the man slapped Papa to the ground and the other men with him kicked Papa again and again. I looked back as that man dragged me into the hall… Papa was so still and Mama was leaning over him, crying and reaching out for me."

"Oh, Marie," LeFeu said, "my poor little angel." If Marie heard her, Monique could not tell. The child was lost in her memory, the story spilling from her like so much foul air. Monique had seen that lost look before – only her sister had never managed to come back from the cage of her memories.

"I don't know where they took me," Marie continued, oblivious to Monique's arms pulling the child up into her lap to hold her tightly. "I had never been very far from my own home before that. It was a big white building with dark halls and dark rooms. They blindfolded me, took me to a room with three other girls. I know the others were there because I could hear them crying and whispering.

"I was tied up all night with a hood over my face. I tried to pray, tried to whisper to the other girls, but as it got later, everything became so scary There was a lot of screaming and shouting that night; I didn't sleep," Marie looked up sheepishly then. "I'm still afraid of the dark, Monique."

LeFeu had no words, she stroked the child's face, meaning to let Marie leave off with this retching of her soul, but Marie soldiered on ready to have the demons of her past purged.

"In the morning, a big woman came to get us and pulled off our hoods. She said if we made any trouble, she would beat us. I could see the other girls then, most of them weren't much bigger than me. The woman threw a pan of bread and a bucket of water into the room, and the others shoved me down getting to those scraps. Some of them looked really dirty, like we did when we arrived on this boat."

LeFeu felt her own twinge of guilt at the remembrance of the water cannons hosing down the frail children. She had gone along with O'Flynn's orders to keep up appearances until she fulfilled her mission.

Marie's words startled LeFeu back to the present. "Later that morning, the woman brought in another bucket, told us all to clean ourselves the best we could. Those who had the worst clothing were given rags not much better and then she led us to another room and told us to line up in front of some men. I tried to hide behind the girl in front of me, but I could still see there were men sitting, talking, drinking tea, laughing on the couches. The girl in front started to cry."

LeFeu bit her lip, trying desperately not to envision the details of Marie's story – not with Marie or with her own sister.

"They told the first girl to stand in the middle of the room. They told her to take off her top, but she didn't do it so a man, the one who took me from my Papa I think, got up from the sofa and slapped her so hard she fell down, then he kicked her really hard. Then that man looked at me; it was my turn. He stood beside me, put his hand inside my shirt and pinched my skin. Then he said, 'Lift up your top."

Monique's hand flew to her mouth to stifle a gasp. Marie mistook her horror at what was done to the child as confirmation that she should be ashamed.

"I lifted my top for a second, but then I pulled it right down," she said hurriedly, echoing the same defiance she must have felt at that moment, as Monique shook her head and pulled the child close. "I would rather die than go with men."

"Oh, little one, I know," Monique assured her. "None of this was your fault. But how did you escape?"

"Behind the sofa, where the men were sitting was a window, and it was open because the cigarette smoke was disappearing out of it. I made up my mind; I remember I said a prayer, 'Oh, God, please help me.' I ran across the room and jumped over the men on the couch and out the window."

That elicited yet another gasp from Monique. "We weren't very high up, and I landed in soft grass under the windowsill and ran as fast as I could. But they caught me, and said I was a 'runner.' After they beat me, they said I was no good for the local market; they were taking me to the market in Zanzibar... to be sold to some Arabs because they like girls with green eyes..."

Marie looked around the luxurious room then. "After a day or two in the room with the crying girls, they took some of us down to the docks and loaded us into the big box, and we wound up here."

She looked up then, her eyes searching Monique's face for acceptance and understanding. "Do you know where Zanzibar is, Monique?"

LeFeu nodded.

"Will you help me, Monique?"

"Yes, I will, my little darling. Yes, I will."

14 COLD AND ALONE

Ari's Niece, Renee

I woke up sad and cold, my knees huddled to my chest. I sat on the floor in a corner of this dark room, as far away from the door as possible.

Today is my twelfth birthday, but none of these nasty people know, and I promised myself I won't tell them.

It has been two weeks since they took me. I've been praying to God to forgive me. I must have done something terrible for Him to want to punish me like this.

The next time my Mama tells me to stay close when we're shopping, I will listen to her. But if only I could go back in time. I should've stayed with my Mama! I saw a stall in the flea market that had the prettiest hats; I know my friends at school would have thought they were really cool.

I walked toward the stall, and suddenly someone grabbed my wrist and pulled me into a dark shop. Then a man – it must have been a man because he was so strong – put a rag over my face. After that, I don't know what happened.

The next thing I remember I woke up cold, with some of my clothes ripped, and I hurt all over my body – in places where I haven't hurt before, and I was bleeding.

At least I have some clothes now. I have heard other kids screaming and crying for help. I don't like this place. I don't know where I am. My Mama and Papa must be worried. I have been praying for Uncle Ari to help me. Mama told me he was in the military. Oh, I hope she has called him! I'm so frightened...

***

The ICU Ward On Board the *Sea Wolfe*

Ari lay unconscious in his bed aboard the *Sea Wolfe*. He was breathing on his own, and Monique sat beside him clutching his right hand, gently stroking the top of his hand and wrist.

She whispered tenderly, "Oh, Ari, I need your help. Please wake up." Her eyes began to tear, and she leaned forward, lifting her two hands with Ari's cupped between them.

"Ari, I spoke to Marie. She needs you. I need you. I knew it in Moscow; I should never have let you go without telling you about my feelings. I think you sensed it, too, but now we both need you." She couldn't help but chuckle half-heartedly, "Marie says God sent you to rescue her; she wants you to be her new Papa."

LeFeu cried openly, tears falling from her eyes so fast she couldn't keep up without a handkerchief. Almost losing control, she tried to remove her hand reaching for a hankie to wipe her eyes. Much louder than she intended, she said, "Oh, Ari, we need—"

Suddenly, she felt the hand holding Ari's gripped tightly, almost painfully, before it was released. Monique jerked upright in surprise, pushing her chair back, still holding Ari's hand. She stood intently looking down at Ari's face, searching for a confirmation she was not mistaken, examining him to see if it was just a muscle spasm or if he was waking up.

Ari's eyes fluttered, and Monique held her free hand to her face, clenching her fist as she bit into her index finger. Then Ari opened his eyes, looked directly up at her, and offered a faint smile. Just as quickly as it happened, his eyes closed and he was limp again. To Monique it didn't matter.

"Doctor! Doctor!" she screamed, "It's Ari; he's waking up!"

On the other side of the ward, Dr. Drakul held a clipboard studying a chart next to the bed of another patient. At first he turned around nonplussed, looking over the rim of his glasses, trying to see the cause of the commotion. As soon as he realized it was Monique standing next to Ari, he replaced the clipboard next to the patient and hurried over to Ari's bed.

He arrived in time to see Ari open his eyes. At first Ari blinked slowly, repeatedly, and deliberately, as if confused, seeing an image he did not expect beside his bed.

Trying to lift his head off his pillow and leaning ever so slightly toward Monique, he whispered softly, "Katarina? Katarina, what… What are you doing here?"

Dr. Drakul stood on the other side of the bed watching the EKG monitor pick up Ari's increasing heartbeat. His face broke into a smile when he confirmed Ari was, in fact, waking up.

Monique leaned over, putting her mouth next to Ari's ear.

"Shush, shoo," she intoned gently, so close to his ear that he was the only person who could hear. "Everybody knows me as Monique here."

15 BRIDGING THE GAP

Monique entered the medical bay with a present for her favorite patient... gripping her hand tightly and promising to be quiet and calm was the effervescent little Marie.

Ari, still weak and tired, but mostly awake when he should be, smiled at both ladies as they came to his bedside. Marie looked up at Monique questioningly, and Ari looked from one to the other puzzled. "Am I missing something?"

"Dr. Drakul warned Marie that she must behave and be quiet in the ward and can't go around flinging herself onto patients," Monique said with a half-smile.

"I see," Ari said, pretending seriousness. "Well, he certainly didn't mean me, but I swear he told me little girls were very good medicine for what I have." He smiled at Marie and held his arms open wide, inviting the inevitable full-force jumping-hug that would rock his still-recovering body. Monique watched him flinch and cringed, but Ari never made a sound of discomfort as Marie launched herself at him and landed square in the middle of his chest.

He nuzzled her like an old pro, and she held on tight. "I told them you would be ok," she whispered into his ear, feeling the scratch of his growing beard against her face. "God would never bring you to me and then take you back."

Ari smiled. "Well, little one, I am very glad you and the Big Guy have such a great understanding of things."

"Me, too," LeFeu said, and Ari noticed something different in how she looked at him.

After only a few minutes of Marie's non-stop chatter, Monique could see the toll it was taking on Ari's depleted reserves. "All right, Angel," she said, lifting the child gently from her perch on the bed next to Ari. "I think we need to give Ari time to rest."

As she started to lead the child out, Dr. Drakul came by with a tray of cookies. "It's snack time on the upper deck. I thought I better make sure my little friend didn't miss it. Want me to take her up?" Monique handed her off thankfully and turned back to Ari's bedside.

He was looking at her with curiosity. They had not had a chance to talk alone since he woke a few days before, and she knew he had questions. Now that his mind was clear, she figured she was about to have to answer them.

Monique settled in next to Ari's bed, leaning in close so that they could speak quietly. "Well, Mr. Cohen, once again you got yourself into a fix and needed me to get you out of it." Her Cheshire Cat smile sent off waves of emotion in Ari, one of which he recognized immediately – that electric connection he had made with Katarina the moment they met.

"So you admit to your double life then?" he said with a smirk. "I knew you looked... familiar."

LeFeu laughed and without realizing it took Ari's hand, a movement that had become too much a habit in the days he was unconscious. When he looked down at their entwined fingers, she held her breath, and when he smiled, something inside her released.

"Familiar. Yes. I knew you the moment I saw you," she said, and as Ari's smile widened, she added, "I never forget a troublemaker."

Ari laughed then, a genuine laugh belying his still fragile condition. The sound rang in Monique's heart.

"Troublemaker? Katarina—"

She quickly held her finger to his lips. "Tut tut… Katarina is no more. Here, I am Monique."

Ari nodded. "Of course, Monique with the French accent rich as honey." Maybe it was the drugs talking or the closeness of death changing his perspective, or maybe it was just being released from the hold Jasmine had held on him when he first met Katarina, whatever it was, he gave in to it and brought her hand up to his lips. "In Russian, your accent purred, but in French you are ever so lovely to listen to."

It was Monique's turn to laugh.

"And your eyes have not changed from one to the other," Ari sighed. "So tell me then, the story of Monique."

Her breath caught. *Was it his lips against the skin of her hand or the thought of telling him who she had become?*

"To everyone I am Monique LeFeu – everyone but my family and the Raven." Torn between the desire to feel his skin on hers and the need to disconnect from him to tell him her story, she finally pulled away and paced a short distance from his bed. Ari sat up straighter against his pillows, intent on her face and trying desperately to send a vibe of acceptance for whatever she might have to say. *There is nothing she could have done that I wouldn't have done in her place.* He instinctively knew he and Katarina – Monique – were too much alike for her to shock him.

She looked at him from underneath her long, dark lashes, her plump dark lips parting to release a sigh. Ari had to force himself to focus on the conversation.

"When you left Russia, you left a wake of trouble behind you." She was not prepared for Ari's look of pain at the thought that whatever had happened to her might be his fault, and she fell back into the seat beside his bed. She took his hand. "We had a job to do, and we did it, but there were consequences, and the people we were dealing with didn't stop at pouring out those consequences on the agents."

Her eyes begged him not to feel guilty, not to add that to her burden. "You and I knew what we were getting into when we signed on with Athena... My sister didn't."

"Your sister?"

"We had no idea at the time that the Bratva had already begun dipping into the human trafficking arena. They now have a network of partners all over the world that either help them ply that trade or purchase from them.

"It took more than a year for them to come looking for revenge on the Russian Athena agents – the three of us who worked with you. Abram and Nestor had no family to speak of, except me, and they died trying to protect me. They managed to secret me away from Moscow and the grasp of the Bratva. I thought my family was safe, but I was wrong.

"They took my sister, meaning to fold her into their sick new sideline of child workers and forced prostitution. Knowing it would draw me out, they made sure her misery was visible to me, hoping I would do something stupid.

"Perhaps, I did," she said with a faraway look in her eyes. "I left Athena – an indefinite leave of absence, although they would never allow me to just vanish from the organization with all I knew. But I still had friends in and out of Athena – good friends with… interesting talents. One of them was the Raven."

She laughed at Ari's surprised look. "Surely you have figured out by now that he isn't half the bad guy you thought he was…" Ari shrugged.

"He helped me become Monique, and together, we managed to take out the crew holding my sister and pimping her out, rescued a half dozen girls from that house, and he scared the Bratva enough that they will not touch Elena again."

"But Athena …?"

"I left to deal with my grief and fell off their radar… Had they wanted to find me, I would have been found."

"Why didn't you call me?"

"Ah, Ari, how little we knew each other then. How could I put my sister's life in the hands of a man I barely knew?"

"I would have come for you, Kat— Monique."

Monique moved her head from side to side, an impish grin on her face, "All I saw of you was a man who took chances. I couldn't risk your mission endangering my sister. If they had found you, they would have killed Elena. The Raven came to me and offered to help. He had been watching you, you see," she said smiling. "He saw what happened in Moscow and the wake of that operation, and he had the connections and the… skills needed to do what we had to do."

"And your sister?"

Monique's face filled with the darkness of buried despair. "She is a shadow of her former self, but I have taken care of the men who did that to her. The Raven helped me, and she is at his sanctuary on Poros; her recovery will take a long time."

Ari again took hold of Monique's hand, and kissed it with the softness of rose petals. "I am sorry, my... French beauty. I would give anything to erase that pain."

She smiled down at him, leaned in and kissed his lips. As she drew back just enough to look into his eyes, she said, "Pain is all I had for so long, erasing it would be to erase me."

He understood, kissed her lips gently and said, "Then I will embrace it – embrace you – for all that you are now."

Monique leaned her brow against his. *Would he still mean that when he knew all that she had become?*

16 BIGGER PREY AT THE LODGE

Vuyani Safari Lodge
Hoedspruit, South Africa

Vuyani Safari Lodge sits in the middle of a private game reserve close to South Africa's Krueger National Park. It was one of those exclusive resorts offering a level of service not measured in mere stars. The staff caters to their guests' every whim, whether it be to spot an elusive leopard, photograph a member of the "big five" or simply hold a meeting, out of sight of any intruders who might try to listen in on a confidential conversation.

Most National Parks in Africa had sign posts hundreds of miles away leading visitors in the right direction. The public is welcome and encouraged to come, whether it be for a day or a week. When visitors arrive at those game reserves, after paying a fee, they are advised to stay in their car, not feed the animals and have a nice day – all very civil. They then drive themselves at their own pace through the park.

Not so at Vuyani, where privacy is treasured, the uninvited, unwelcome. On a lonely stretch of R40 in South Africa's North East Veld, drivers might see many things – 15-foot wire fences, fruit stands, a few road signs (some warning against feeding baboons), but no markers with directions to Vuyani Safari Lodge. If travelers don't know the way, they aren't invited. Those invited who didn't know the way found a private limousine sent to fetch them.

An entourage of ten limousines had been sent for the current lodge guests. As they pulled up to the lodge entrance, they waited in line for the armed escort to arrive. "Big Daddy T," the boss of the African syndicate, had called a meeting. He was leaving his sanctuary in Stone Town, Zanzibar, to talk in person to his lieutenants.

The big man rarely left his base, but when he did, he wanted to be pampered and he wanted luxury. His favorite locale? Vuyani Safari Lodge.

As they awaited their escort, the group of unsavory characters inside the limos took stock of the area around them. The only clue of any proximity to Vuyani had been the sight of the majestic Drakensberg Mountain Range on one side of R40 and the infamous Timbavati Game Reserve to the east.

The Drakensberg Mountains marked the territory of KwaZulu-Natal, the territory of South Africa's most feared tribe. Zulus had long called this range of lush yellowwood forests and cascading waterfalls home. In the winter, the snow-capped peaks gave rise to the Zulu name for Drakensberg, the Barrier of Spears.

Zulu warriors have been proud, fearless fighters since the beginning of recorded history – as the British found out, much to their surprise, toward the end of the nineteenth century in Rorke's Drift. Hundreds of years later, even the hardened criminals of "Big Daddy T's" crew knew enough to be wary of the Zulus.

Had they not had limo drivers sent from the lodge, the crew would never have found their way. Across the road from a mile marker with the number long rubbed off, sat the entrance to Vuyani. Some say the mile marker number was licked off by salt-craving antelope; others say Vuyani management were guilty due to their almost obsessive desire for privacy. But no matter, the mile marker was barren.

The entrance was guarded around the clock. Uniformed employees keep watch through one-way glass windows on all who might approach. Every visitor's identity was verified by a call to the main lodge. If the visitor was approved, a four-wheel-drive escort with armed guards was dispatched from the lodge to escort the new arrivals in safety.

Once inside the gate, GPS wouldn't work; no signs marked the way to the lodge, and motorized vehicle tracks and old game trails crisscrossed the entire reserve. It was "Enter alone at your own peril." Getting lost or running into a steaming fresh heap of elephant dung were both high-probability risks.

Later that Night....

In a dusty, smoke shrouded area of the Vuyani Safari Lodge sits a traditional Boma. A Boma is a term used to describe a livestock enclosure or a stockade, sometimes a small fort that is found in many parts of the African plains.

The safari lodge had converted a traditional Boma into a private, fenced conference area, open to the night. The sky above filled with a cacophony of stars, their bright light almost illuminating the Boma. In the middle sits a large concrete base on which a fire blazed.

Around the fire lounge chairs were arranged in a circle. Behind those chairs an open bar manned by two Askari. Wax candles glowed inside glass covers placed prominently down the middle of the rectangular dinner table made out of aged and polished kiaat, a local wild teak like tree.

On the opposite side of the Boma from the table, sat a traditional South African barbecue cooking area, hot coals glowing in the darkening night. Sitting in the chairs around the fire, 14 men sit, nursing cocktails.

Thorny acacia enclosed the Boma, protecting those inside from the fangs of predators. Conversation around the circular fire pit was light, not so outside. Off in the distance a roar came out of the deep canopy, the intensity so spine chilling it spilled more than than a few cocktails. It was the voice and sound of Africa, sending an awesome message to all that the lord and master of this area was very close and this was his domain.

Inside the conference center, frightened eyes widened, guests looked from one to another in uncertainty. The Askari watched amused, making light of their guest's reactions. But their knuckles whitened, they clenched their Assegai more tightly, the primitive horror provoked by one of Africa's most feared predators. The guests tried to ignore the rising bile in their throats, but the Askari remained unmoved, but they had their spears.

"Lion?" Shouted one of the guests to the Askari.

In a deep baritone he simply responded, "Lionsssss."

As if to emphasis his response, the first lions soft rumble was followed by a ferocious roar from the other side of the Boma. All the guests as one, turned, as if watching a tennis match, to look at the other side of the Boma from where the new roar had come. Another lion responded with more low pitched rumbles followed by a series of grunts.

By now all the Lieutenants were looking over to the Askari as if asking for confirmation that two guards, holding skinny spears were enough protection from the pride that were close by. The Askari simply shook his head, signaling what, no one knew.

With much trepidation in his voice, another asked, "Is it safe to walk back to our rooms?"

"No." Came the response, without elaborating.

The guards were enjoying their guest's discomfort, he hesitated just long enough to make certain the level of fear was rising.

"When you have finished dinner we will call for the Landrovers to come escort you back to the main lodge." The primitive fear of being in the king of the jungle's domain and out of their own comfort zone etched on more than one face. Suddenly the effect of too many cocktails disappeared.

"Will we be safe during the night?"

"We have Askari that patrol all night, but don't go outside to smoke a cigarette."

Another asked, "Do you smell it?"

"What?" As if on queue, a light breeze came into the Boma, bearing the sweet, pungent, unmistakeable smell of rotting meat.

"You will be safe tonight, they have eaten."

"I'll be glad when Tippu gets here. This place gives me the creeps."

The Capos of the African/European child trafficking cartel were assembled, waiting for the arrival of one person.....

***

"Captain to the bridge, please! Captain to the bridge!" The voice bellowed over the *Sea Wolfe's* comm system, startling many of the personnel aboard. O'Flynn was in his cabin still feeling a little groggy after waking up from his afternoon siesta.

He made a grab for the ship's service telephone, shouted into the receiver, and after receiving no answer, turned the phone over as if expecting to see a display indicating why no one was responding. Fearing there might be a problem with the equipment, he dropped the ship's telephone handset and made another grab for the stand-by Voice Tube System.

O'Flynn shouted into the tube, "This is the Captain; what's the emergency?" O'Flynn put the tube to his ear, waiting for an answer. It was quiet. Fearing the worst, he hurried out of his cabin without brushing his hair or getting his Captain's hat.

Nautical traditional design always prefers a captain's cabin be fairly close to the bridge – just in case – the *Sea Wolfe* was no exception. Slamming his cabin door behind him, he trotted down the passageway, flying through the bridge door and skidding to a stop in front of three people.

The Raven, Major Monique LeFeu and Ari Cohen were lined up with their backs to the bow of the ship, side by side, waiting for the captain to arrive. O'Flynn looked around the bridge. Seeing no other officers, he halted, confused. Stangl didn't wait for O'Flynn to wonder very long.

"Sit down, O'Flynn." The Raven pointed to a seat that had been pulled close to where the captain was standing. A long pause ensued, with the

Raven, LeFeu and Ari staring at O'Flynn. Slowly comprehension spread over the captain's face.

"I think you know why we called you up here, O'Flynn. You have one choice: tell us what we want to know or I will tell Major LeFeu to get the information out of you… privately, one on one, if you get my drift. Your choice."

The captain was not a courageous man; he withered in front of them. Looking from side to side, he shuffled anxiously to his seat. A man used to scheming his whole life, he didn't respond immediately, racking his brain for a way out. Finally, convinced they knew about his former occupation, he wiped his eyes and took his time, looking at each face in front of him.

"What is it you want to know?" the former captain of the *Sea Wolfe* finally asked with confidence he didn't feel.

Ari watched O'Flynn intently; he didn't like the vibes he was getting. As O'Flynn asked the question, he had his index finger bent over the tip of his nose, rubbing the bottom of his nose with the soft side of his right thumb, as if scheming, *"How can I get out of this?* And *How much do they know?*

"Names of your bosses, routes, customers, safe houses, everything," the Raven said firmly. O'Flynn didn't pause long before responding nervously.

"I was only involved in the African operation, trade routes, people. I will tell you everything if you guarantee me a safe sanctuary to live out my remaining years."

Ari was guilt-ridden; he couldn't help but think he should have done more to save Renee before she was moved. The bridge was silent, no one spoke, but the tension was thick. He reached behind his back and pulled his Glock from the rear of his belt. He surprised the Raven and LeFeu, their concern not quite hidden on stoic faces. All eyes were on him; they didn't know what he planned, but by now, they both knew him well enough to recognize the look on his face.

Ari kept his eyes riveted on O'Flynn, as his hands worked mechanically from memory. He pulled back the slide, revealing the barrel. He turned it to one side and clicked the catch, releasing the magazine. The well-oiled mechanism slid out. Ari pulled the magazine out, checked the bullets, then re-loaded them, before re-inserting the magazine back into the body of the gun.

The slide pulled back effortlessly, releasing a bullet into the breach. O'Flynn looked constipated. He gripped the sides of his seat with white knuckles, his eyes wide in fear, afraid to utter a word.

Ari spoke in a low voice, hissing like a cobra, "Some of your cohorts have my niece..." Then in an even more menacing voice, "You think I'm going to negotiate with you?"

O'Flynn swallowed hard; he didn't know what to say. Ari lifted his Glock, and without consciously aiming, he pointed the gun at O'Flynn's knee.

"Okay, okay!" O'Flynn pleaded, lifting his hands from his seat, palms out as if to protect his body from the lead projectiles that might be discharged from Ari's weapon.

Stammering, begging, he said, "I don't know your niece; I only arranged the transportation."

Ari struggled with his emotions... O'Flynn was overcome with fear from the thought that he was about to receive a bullet in the knee...The Raven and LeFeu were mesmerized by the scene, watching Ari, seeing a side of him they had not known existed.

"You are lucky you don't know her name." Ari's gun hand shook ever so slightly with emotion he was suppressing, his face taught with revulsion. "If her name was to pass your foul lips..." Ari had to turn away from the monster in front of him.

As he turned, LeFeu crouched catlike, right arm extended supported by her left hand gripping her right forearm. In her grip, a stun gun was leveled at O'Flynn.

In micro-seconds, a high-voltage, low-current electrical discharge barreled across the short distance in the bridge from Monique's stun gun toward O'Flynn. He didn't have time to react before the two metal probes entered his left shoulder, the wires delivering a thunderous charge of electricity. Every muscle in O'Flynn's body seemed to stretch tight, his relaxed arms and legs suddenly kicking out in front of him, twitching uncontrollably.

It was his eyes that showed the pain he was feeling. The muscles in his eyelids pulled back taught exposing so much of the eyeballs they seemed they might just roll out. As quickly as the shock had been delivered, it was over, leaving a stunned and sweat-covered former captain gripping the side of his seat to avoid falling to the floor.

LeFeu reined in her weapon, pulled another cartridge from her belt, and reloaded before aiming again for O'Flynn. His eyes pleaded with her, his tongue so traumatized by the shock it rolled uncontrollably from side to side and made it difficult to mouth any response.

"What's your boss's name and where is he?" LeFeu asked so calmly that her words carried even more weight than if she'd shouted them.

"Tippu Tip; he is known as 'Big Daddy T.' I don't know where he is now. He lives in a fortress outside of Stone Town, Zanzibar."

17 LOST AT SEA

Renee, Somewhere At Sea

I wish Gareth was here with me. I was so mean to him before. I wonder what day it is? I am below decks on a very smelly boat. I hear no engine noise, so it must be a dhow. Papa used to take me out on a yacht, but I never imagined a yacht being so dirty. At night, I hear scratching sounds; I hope they aren't rats, but that's what Gareth told me they were before they took him away. I think he was just trying to frighten me.

We are in a storage hold, I guess, because we're sitting on stacks of mangrove tree logs and barrels of dried fish. That must be why it smells so bad, old fish and vomit. Some of the children in here are sick almost every day. It wouldn't be so bad if we had a bathroom – or some fresh air. We can't even see outside – just tiny rays of light shining through some gaps in the walls.

Gareth told me he thought he saw a sign through one little hole that said "Port Said." He said that means we were going through the Suez Canal and that was why it was so calm. But that was before we hit rough seas and many of us were seasick again.

Gareth was worried; he told me who these horrible men were. He said they were slavers, probably taking us to market to be sold. After he told me that, he said these men might come down here to get one of us, "for their entertainment." I know what he means; I still ache from the last time they hurt me in France. But Gareth and I made a pact, if they came to get one of us, we would try to escape, jump overboard, try to stay afloat until another ship came by. We knew we had to do something.

It wasn't me they came for, it was Gareth. These sailors unshackled him, saying something neither of us understood, and took him out, but as he was leaving, manhandled by these brutes, he looked back at me and winked. Then he struggled free for just a minute, smiled that big goofy smile and managed to squeeze out, "I'll get help."

The men slapped him real hard across the head, and he nearly fell down. I could tell he was hurt, but he tried not to show it. The men dragged him up and away. Then it was very quiet for a while as they walked back up to the main deck. The sounds of the boat swooshing through the sea returned. A few minutes later, I heard men laughing and I heard Gareth shout something, then I heard a big splash. All of a sudden, the men on board were shouting very loudly. I couldn't understand what they said, but the ship didn't stop or turn around. I think Gareth jumped overboard. Oh, I hope he is alright. I'm so frightened.

That was two days ago; I haven't heard or seen anyone since. Gareth has not come back. But now something is different; I hear the excited noise of seabirds as they fly around the boat. I hadn't noticed their absence before. It must mean we are getting close to land. The overpowering stench of fish and human waste is now mingled with something new, a sweet smell. I heard the noise of rope screeching its way through a rusty pulley, then the flapping sound of a sail as it was released from its hold on the wind. We must be slowing down.

I know what that smell is! It reminds me of my mother's apple pie. I am so hungry, my tummy is rumbling. Oh, where am I? Where is my Mama? I'm so frightened.

***

The *Sea Wolfe*
Somewhere in the Mediterranean

Rafik waited two long years for this moment. He had counted the days, marking each day off on his calendar in the cramped, smelly quarters aboard the *Sahara*. He never imagined the captain's quarters on any seagoing vessel could be this primitive. His cabin was wedged between the galley and the engine room. That meant he either stank of diesel or greasy food.

When he agreed to "temporarily" vacate his position as captain on the

Sea Wolfe, he had no idea it would be for this long. After months of searching, following hundreds of leads, their shipping agent in Athens had radioed the Raven that they received a confidential inquiry from a high-ranking member of the African slave trade looking for an out.

Further inquiries indicated this person hoped to find a position as a captain of an ocean-going vessel. Stangl wanted to have access to this person, gain his confidence and learn everything he could about the slavers. The only problem – he was only just starting out on his quest for vengeance; Stangl didn't even know enough yet to ask the right questions.

It was Taman, himself, who thought of the idea. Many times over the following two years, he wished he had held his tongue. But Taman offered his idea up to the Raven – offered his job to O'Flynn, offered his command as captain to a complete stranger. Over the months that followed, the more they learned about this slave trade, the more difficult it was to rationalize their decision. Before long, both Taman and Stangl wished they could end this reprobate's life and feed him to the sharks, but he still had valuable information and didn't know they were on to him.

O'Flynn was no ring-leader, his arrogance and ignorance made that clear, but he had managed to use brute force to work his way up the syndicate food chain – mostly by eating the smaller fish along the way. Once he was dealing with the big boys, he found himself a guppy in a shark tank and needed an escape. Stangl knew O'Flynn had the information they would need when the time was right – if they could stomach him that long – and so they had.

But when Taman received word from the Raven to come on home, he could hardly contain his happiness. The very thought of trashing the disguise he had been wearing for two years filled him with joy.

Taman sat in Stangl's chopper flying low over the Indian Ocean. In the distance, he could see the outline of the *Sea Wolfe* becoming more and more visible, and the closer he got, the bigger his smile became. *It is time,* he thought to himself. He stretched his right hand over to the left side of his face and reached by his ear as his fingers searched for the edge of the mask he had been forced to wear.

His fingers found the edge, and with glee he ripped the mask with the ugly scar from his face. He reached up again to pull off a few surviving pieces, then shook his head in relief to be finally free of his restraining subterfuge.

***

A helicopter hovering low over the sea has its own distinct signature. The vibration of the air forced down onto the surface of the sea at warp speed seemed to reverberate or echo, as if making the skin tingle in anticipation. As the *Sea Wolfe* chopper approached the Raven's yacht, it descended from 100 feet above the sea to circle the bow before landing. Stangl monitored its approach from the bridge.

As it prepared to land, he put the radio transmitter to his mouth, "Took you long enough to get here, Rick. What was the hold up?"

On board the chopper, the only passenger grabbed the radio, leaned to the side to look out the window at the *Sea Wolfe*, and half-smiling, shouted back, trying to be heard over the thunderous noise of the helicopter, "Don't you ever ask me to captain the *Sahara* again. The food on that tub is so bad I've lost 25 pounds."

"A few months of rationing didn't do you any harm, my old friend. Anyway, welcome home," Stangl said playfully. "I'll meet you in my quarters. We have much to do, and time is short. I want to introduce you to the guy who nearly blew your cover at the Black Cat."

"He's here?" Captain Rick Tanner's response was interrupted by the Bell 206 Jetranger banking sharply to prepare to land on the deck of the *Sea Wolfe*. Minutes later he exited the chopper and stood still on the pad, just enjoying the moment, as if he was being reunited with a long lost love. He took one last look at his command before hurrying below decks to meet with the Raven.

18 GARETH FOUND

Reuters: Boy Found Clinging to Debris at Sea

ZANZIBAR − A U.S. Navy drone on patrol off the coast of Ethiopia in the Indian Ocean alerted authorities to the perilous condition of a young boy lost at sea Saturday.

Due to the increase in piracy of commercial freighters and oil tankers in the corridor between Africa and the Middle East, the U.S. Navy actively monitors any suspicious activity in the area. On a recent fly-by, a drone took video of what was at first thought to be a small pirate boat. After the video was relayed back to base, further analysis discovered the vessel in question was, in fact, a makeshift raft floating in the ocean with only one person aboard.

An alert was immediately broadcast to all ships in the area to be on the lookout for what could be either a man overboard from a capsized vessel or perhaps something more nefarious. Any ships spotting the craft were asked to approach with caution and rescue the lone survivor if he was determined not to be a threat.

A luxury yacht, the Sea Wolfe answered the call. Fortunately the yacht had a doctor on board who was able to treat the castaway for a severe case of exposure and dehydration.

It was discovered the boy, whose identity is being withheld pending notification of his family, had jumped overboard from an Arab dhow to escape captors taking him to an unknown destination, reportedly to sell him into slavery. Although he spent more than two days drifting on the open sea, the doctor on board said the boy is expected to make a full recovery.

The boy was found 55 nautical miles north of Zanzibar, where the victim thinks he was being taken together with a consignment of other kidnapped children held captive on the dhow.

Chief Assistant Director Nicole Gautier, of Interpol's Human Trafficking and Child Exploitation Division, said, "I will move heaven and earth to find these children and punish the perpetrators."

***

Lyons, France

Thirteen miles southeast of Lyons, at Saint Exupéry Airport, David Gray's plane prepared to land. His body was still on Washington, DC, time, and he had been sleeping fitfully when the steward's voice and gentle shaking of his shoulder penetrated his slumber. Gray opened his eyes, blinking to clear the sleep. "What is it?"

"We'll be on the ground in five minutes, sir. The captain thought you might like a few moments to get ready before we land."

"Yes, thank you. Got any coffee?" Gray stretched in his seat, trying to shake the jet lag. He turned to the window, pushed up the blind, and blinked as the light suddenly blinded him. As his eyes grew accustomed to the new day, he stared out through the Plexiglas window, his mind vividly replaying his conversation with Jade.

His beautiful wife, the President of the United States, had asked him for a favor. As soon as he agreed, he was on his way, rushed to Andrews Air Force base to hitch a ride to France, after a quick visit to the "nest," he and the President maintained at Blair House.

Thinking back, he had rarely seen such unbridled emotion on his wife's face. Gray knew she had a soft spot for children, but to actually see tears stream down her cheeks...

Sometimes, his life roles became a bit confusing. He was assigned to Jade McQueen some years back as the head of her personal security detail when she was Secretary of State. Then something happened, and their relationship had become more personal than he could have imagined. As she became Vice President, they became engaged. Before she became President, they were married. He was no longer officially part of her Secret Service detail, but he had never given up the job of protecting her.

Gray struggled to bring his mind back to the current assignment. She didn't have to push hard to get his agreement. Ari needed assistance finding his niece – before he got himself into any more trouble. David wished Ari had asked for help. *One of these days, his go-it-alone style could get him killed.*

In truth, Ari had been more distant since the break-up with Jasmine. He had thought her the love of his life, and they had gone through hell and back together. But in the end, Jasmine's torture at the hands of Wolfgang Stangl was too much for them to overcome. She needed stability and peace that she'd never get with a boyfriend who spent his working hours chasing bad guys all over the world. It had crushed them both, but letting go had been the best thing for Jasmine, and Ari loved her too much not to do that for her.

Gray thought back to the early days in his friendship with Ari. He owed him everything; Ari had saved his life in Yugoslavia and had saved Jade's life, as well. They were a family now, a bond that only grew stronger with each mission they undertook, and Jade was always right in the middle of it.

A jarring thud shook Gray from his thoughts; his plane had touched down. He was in a C-32, a military version of the Boeing 757-200 extended range aircraft, supplied courtesy of the U.S. Air Force. With an effort, he readjusted his eyes to look beyond the Plexiglas cabin window. A lone black suburban sped away from the private terminal coming toward his plane.

Moments later, Gray was in the back seat of the suburban alone. He thought ahead to his coming visit at Interpol, wondering what that organization could tell him. As much as he tried to plan that agenda, he couldn't shake the thought that his best friend needed him. He reached into his pocket and pulled out his phone.

As soon as Ari answered, Gray could tell everything was weighing on him. Gone was the normally happy greeting he received.

Caller ID must have identified Gray calling, but that didn't lift Ari's response. It was a cheerless voice that answered, "Hello, David."

"No luck on Renee yet, Ari?"

"All I have is the story of the young boy we picked up at sea. I think he was in the same boat as Renee, and he thinks the dhow was making for Zanzibar. Not much to go on is it?"

"Ari, I'm pulling up in front of Interpol now. I'll call you when I'm done; I'll see if they can shed any light on Zanzibar for you."

***

The International Criminal Police Organization, or Interpol, a non-governmental organization facilitating international police cooperation, was the second largest international agency after the United Nations.

Established as the International Criminal Police Commission in 1923, its work focused primarily on terrorism, crimes against humanity, genocide, atrocities of war, organized crime and piracy. Lyon, halfway between Paris and Marseille, was its home base.

Many thought of Interpol as something akin to the CIA or M16. Over the years, it had been associated with spies and international espionage, and its Ten Most Wanted list included murderers, art thieves and drug lords. However, most of Interpol's work was focused on protecting the innocent. In fact, one entire department was dedicated to the war against child slavery.

Deep inside Interpol's Lyon headquarters, dedicated case workers looked into all aspects of real human suffering. They examined records of workers all over the globe – even on U.S. construction sites and farms, restaurants and hotels, and those working in the homes of the super wealthy.

Many foreign workers were lured by false promises of good jobs and a new life only to find themselves enslaved as victims of labor trafficking. Most were unable to report their plight to the authorities for fear of deportation, their children often kidnapped for short periods by their captors to entertain sick sexual pedophiles participating in wild, drug-laced orgies.

Interpol's reach even spread to Asia, where studies concluded one in three electronic workers was forced to work under slave-like conditions.

The largest department within this investigative arm of Interpol was dedicated to crimes against children, not only child pornography, but also sexual slavery, kidnapping, and, most recently, trafficking in body parts. Children were kidnapped and their DNA and blood profiles kept in a computerized data bank, waiting for a match to a wealthy customer in need of a transplanted heart, liver, kidney, lung, or bone marrow. All were available.

When a match was triggered, it was no longer necessary to send the organ in a refrigerated container. Instead, the living child was sedated and transported to the surgical center where the transplant would be performed.

After the donor had the organ in question removed, any other parts of value were also taken, refrigerated and sent to various other transplant centers worldwide. The body of the donor – the victim of organ trafficking – was never seen again.

Gray didn't know how McQueen had done it, but they had laid out the red carpet for him. No sooner had his Suburban pulled up in front of the headquarters of Interpol than he was escorted across the lobby into an elevator and taken to an expansive office.

He only had time to glance briefly at the name plate on the door before it was opened for him by his escort. *Chief Assistant Director Nicole Gautier, Human Trafficking and Child Exploitation.*

"Here we are, monsieur." Gray's escort turned with a very slight bow, "the director."

Behind the desk. Gautier returned her phone to its cradle, waving Gray over. As she looked up, he noticed compassionate, sad brown eyes inspecting him. Her auburn hair was pulled back tight over her head, secured in a bun. Her no-nonsense, business-like impression was mellowed by the saddest of smiles, as if her occupation and the knowledge of the evil she battled weighed heavily on her.

Confirming Gray's first impression as he sat in front of her desk, she said with no preamble, "I had no idea your President was interested in our work here. God knows we could use the influence of the White House." Although her eyes exuded warmth, her face showed little emotion, all business.

Gray looked around her office. On the wall was a large world map with different colored pins, and to the side hundreds of photographs of children of all ages.

Gautier followed his gaze, "Every morning, I look at that map; I add a few pins, mark the location of the latest kidnappings, add a photograph if I have one of the victim. It helps me keep focused."

Gray looked from the map back to the director. He could see the internal conflict ripping her apart. One moment a harsh, no-nonsense, enraged look when she contemplated the barbarians kidnapping children, and then the compassionate look of a mother suckling her newborn when she thought of the victims.

She turned to face Gray, her eyes focusing directly on him. Her voice lowered a pitch, matching her sadness, almost as if she were choking up. "You see, Mr. Gray, we are overwhelmed. Sometimes, we sit here with a good idea of where a child is being taken or abused, but we lack the resources to do anything about it.

"This trafficking in children is a multi-billion dollar business for international organized crime. It is modern-day slavery. My department looks into the worst, most despicable of crimes – trafficking children for sexual exploitation and the murder or maiming of children for their organs. A kidney fetches $50,000, a lung $75,000."

Gray watched her, her fists clenched tightly, her lips pursed as if she were doing everything she could to maintain control of her emotions.

She took her eyes from Gray and looked at the map on the wall. As if dreaming of her wish list, she added wistfully,

"I just need a secret weapon. If... if only we had a guardian angel."

Then her face hardened again and she spat out with venom, "But a guardian angel with the power of Thor – to seek revenge, to make these monsters suffer, to put them out of business permanently."

Gray was shocked by the intensity of her outburst. He took a deep breath and nodded his head slightly, understanding now. It finally all made sense. Now he knew why McQueen had sent him.

Ari Cohen, Jade McQueen and David Gray had just been officially re-commissioned. He realized that sometimes, just sometimes, the White House could achieve more going through unofficial channels. The Eye from New York, the first female President of the United States and the most powerful woman on the planet, had just sanctioned the official involvement of the Eyes of Athena in the quest to rid the world of child trafficking. Gray knew what he had to do. For the first time since he left Washington, he felt good. He had that resolute feeling in the pit of his stomach; the trio had found a cause to champion.

He felt a smile spread across his face. "Madame Director, I have some news for you; I bring you greetings from **Thor**... his earthly name is..... Ari Cohen."

Gautier sat stock-still. Other than the surprise on her face, she made no movement except with her eyes. Her stare penetrated deep into Gray's, trying to decide if this was the typical White House bravado or in fact sincere words being conveyed directly from the President of the United States.

Finally, she finished her assessment. "Good, because I know the man you seek; he is number one on my department's Most Wanted List. He goes by the name Tippu Tip, and no one knows his real name. The head of the Zanzibar trafficking cartel is always called by the name of the original founder, even though that man has been dead for decades. Rumor has it he is scheduled to meet his lieutenants in South Africa this week."

"Do you know where?"

"Vuyani Safari Lodge. When Tippu Tip leaves his fortress outside of Stone Town, he demands the best, not only in food and accommodations, but also security. Vuyani has the best natural security force in the world – the largest pride of Africa's most feared predator. In Swahili the word is still whispered with the greatest of respect, *Simba*."

19 CINNAMON SHORES

The old dhow bumped gently up against the dock, and Renee heard the excited chatter of sailors shouting orders in some language she didn't understand.

She inhaled deeply through her nose. "I know that smell." She couldn't help herself, she blurted out loudly. "It's cinnamon. Mon Dieu, where am I?"

Tears began to stream down her cheeks again. "Oh, Mama, Ari, please come help me, please... I'm so frightened."

Renee slumped back onto the barrel she was sitting on. She rested her face in the palm of her hands, overcome with grief. Slowly the angst of her situation overwhelmed her and she asked herself, shaking her head in confusion. *"What's next?"*

***

During the height of the slave trade in Zanzibar, kidnapped slaves were brought to Stone Town from as far away as Central Africa for auction. Upon arrival, they were taken to slave chambers underground in the center of Stone Town, close to the whipping post.

The abominable treatment of these unfortunate victims in the chambers below the city was followed by being hog-tied to the whipping post so that movement was impossible, then whipped unmercifully by a slave master. If the slave cried or screamed, the value decreased. A slave who did not cry out after prolonged imprisonment in the chamber and the subsequent whipping was deemed more valuable than a screamer; in theory, they would be harder workers.

After the abolition of slavery in Zanzibar, the Anglican Church was built where the whipping post had stood. The Cathedral took ten years to build, constructed largely out of local coral stone. In fact, in an ironic turn of events, the demand for coral stone to feed the area's building boom was so intense that many subterranean caves and passageways were carved out and left behind for the enterprising locals to use. Despite the slavery ban, the continued demand for slaves meant this underground network was soon put to use in the illicit trade in human bondage.

The underground caves became routes for slavers and chambers for slaves, specially adapted for holding these innocent victims prior to transportation. Some three kilometers north of Stone Town lay two large sloping stone slabs, just above ground level. These were once roofs covering a set of small underground rooms in which more than 100 slaves would be packed, awaiting the arrival of the merchant ships to steal them away.

In the twenty-first century, the descendants of Tippu Tip continued this despicable use of these tunnels, but the human trafficking business had been reversed. Now captives were being landed at the old departure point and herded into the slave chambers. Most came from Europe.

***

The boat came to a stop, banging up against a dock, throwing Renee from her makeshift stool with a violent shock. She went to the outside wall of her prison to peak through a small gap, in time to see one of the guards leap on shore, pulling a rope that creaked as it tightened to moor the boat to the landing jetty. Petrified, Renee felt sure this was the end of her voyage.

She turned as she heard the banging of heavy footsteps on the iron walkway outside her cell. The door was thrust open so suddenly that she jumped. A guard filled the doorway, one thin, pale arm held in his hand belonging to a child dragged along behind him.

"You, come!" the guard bellowed in broken English. When Renee did not immediately comply, his scowl deepened. "Come, now!" He reached for a short truncheon on his belt, and Renee forced herself to break the fear that froze her in her tracks and move forward for the sake of her life.

When she drew close, he stepped back into the gangway, pointing for her to step ahead of him heading toward the upper decks. She saw the figure of a frail girl dangling from the limp arm in his grasp. Only a couple years younger than Renee, her eyes were vacant, her jaw slack.

Renee realized the guard did not drag the girl to force her to follow but simply to keep her upright and moving.

When they reached the top deck and neared the gangway, the guard tossed his rag doll onto a pile of ripped sheeting and grabbed Renee by the arm, tossing her to the dock. Before she could stand, he pitched his other captive after Renee, knocking her from her knees back onto her belly. Renee struggled to get up, pushing the other unmoving child off, as she made ready to stand up.

The guard grabbed them both then – their thin arms easily fitting into one of his massive palms. He then dragged them toward a flight of small stone steps, nearly overgrown with vegetation, leading up a slight incline.

Renee wondered where the other children were. She made no attempt to resist the brute. He soon swapped hands so that he held one captive on each side. Renee falling in line with the little ghost on his other side, she felt powerless to resist.

As if in a third dimension, she dragged one foot after the other as she was bid. At the top of the hill, they stopped in front of two large stone slabs on the ground, enough space between them for a man to squeeze through. The guard unceremoniously shoved the smaller girl through the gap, then pulled Renee closer and pushed her forward.

Now, she resisted with a vengeance. Her heart told her this was her last chance before entering purgatory. She punched her guard in the stomach; he didn't even flinch, but for the first time she saw the most evil of smiles creep across his face, as if he enjoyed her panic.

The guard raised his massive hand and released it toward her head. Renee flew toward the gap between the rocks and fell the small distance to the bottom. In a semi-conscious state, she felt her jailer land on his feet beside her and sensed him still smiling evilly.

To Renee it all felt like a dream. She was tempted to speak – to talk to her guard, appeal to his sense of humanity. Her forehead was already beaded with salty sweat, dripping down her nose onto her tongue as she tried to moisten her cracked lips. The humidity was overbearing; the pitiful rags she wore, sopping wet. The musty, damp smell invoked images of dungeons she had visited as a tourist earlier in the summer.

The guard grabbed her by the hair and pulled her to her feet beside his other captive. Both were bloodied from the fall, but the child's eyes still showed no connection with the world around her. He shoved them both down the dark tunnel.

The floor of the tunnel had been rubbed smooth by the countless other feet that had preceded her. The ceiling hung low, forcing her guard to crouch. Despite her diminutive size, she also leaned forward as she stumbled on. The only light came from a kerosene lamp the guard carried, casting dark shadows on the floor in front of them.

She tried to look over her shoulder at the jailer behind her, but was afraid to turn too far toward him. He looked more like a monster than anything she had ever seen. She was convinced there was not an ounce of humanity in his soul. She thought he looked Arabic with a hooked nose and dark complexion. One ear appeared to have been sliced off vertically. On what remained of his ear, he wore a large, gold, hoop earring, pinned unnaturally almost to the inner part because of the missing lobe. It added to his ghoulish appearance.

He shoved both girls forward without a word. The smile had been replaced by a smirk equally as evil. Renee had neither the power nor the will to resist. She stumbled forward, not knowing where she found the strength to continue. The guard pushed her toward an old, heavy oak door to one side of the tunnel, which swung open on rusted hinges. As she pushed the door further open, it creaked noisily. The girl beside her continued through the door, mounted the few steps just inside and was immediately pushed down onto a three-legged stool as the guard held Renee by the arm beside him.

Renee tried desperately to see what was happening to the girl – what would happen to her. As she crooked her head around her guard's massive side, his face was suddenly even with hers – dark, cold eyes inches from her own. "Do not move."

He turned back to the zombie-like girl on the stool. She stared straight ahead as he moved to her side, grabbed hold of her right arm and secured it under his arm pit. As he did so, Renee heard a voice from behind his gigantic form in front of her.

"Hold her tight," the stranger said in a very matter-of-fact tone. As the guard readjusted his grip, Renee thought she caught a glimpse of a filthy white lab coat covered in blood stains. All she could see was the girl, her arm disappearing into the guard's form.

She jumped when the silent child cried out, "Ow!"

The guard released her arm for a moment, and when she withdrew it, she rubbed at her bleeding finger. After a few moments, the voice in the darkness beyond the guard said, "Type AB, good. Mahrook, take her to *the* room."

Her captor had a name now, and the knowledge sent a chill down her spine. She thought to run back the way they had come – back through the still open doorway – but was totally blindsided when she felt Mahrook's grip on her shoulder. She had not seen him turn.

As he did, Renee could see the table of needles and vials of blood. Beyond was a door open on a makeshift cavern clinic visible because of its light against the dark vault in which they now stood. The beds all held small forms. The man in the lab coat was dragging the small girl through the door.

"Take her. See that she is prepared." Renee did not know what he meant, but she felt terror for the child. Then she realized the man in the coat was back in the chamber and she was the girl on the stool.

She bit the hand on her shoulder and ran toward the open doorway. As she reached the first step, she felt Mahrook's huge palm around the back of her neck. He yanked her backward forcefully and slammed her against the rock wall.

As her consciousness faded, she heard the man in the lab coat speak. "I can see why they sent her to Stone Town, but she is far too pretty for the knife. We will try the whip first – teach her to be a good little girl."

***

Much later, Renee woke with a crashing headache. She opened her eyes gingerly, trying to get her bearings. She quickly realized she was being carried deeper into the underground. A chill ran down her spine and she felt the cool sweaty skin of the person carrying her, his bare shoulders and reeking body odor repugnant to her.

Gradually her eyes grew accustomed to the darkness. Something was swinging in front of her face. It gleamed brightly whenever a haze of light shone on it from the lantern in his hand – a large, gold earring, hanging from the grotesquely distorted ear of Mahrook.

Her terror suddenly overwhelmed her and she screamed, the sound barely audible from her parched throat, and without a word Mahrook laid her on the stone floor.

"Where is the girl?" Renee couldn't help but demand the answer. "What did you do to her?"

She got no response as her jailer turned around and disappeared, closing the door behind him and taking with him the lamp, the sudden deafening silence interrupted only by water dripping from the walls of her prison cell.

Renee began to scream. She couldn't help herself. "Where is the girl?! What have you done to her?" She repeated the questions over and over in an ever increasing pitch, her terror rising with the fervor of her pleas.

When she heard the voice in the darkness, a voice of utter despair, emotionless. Renee's mind snapped. "The girl is dead. Be good, or they'll kill you, too."

20 SPLITTING UP

Gray gently closed the door to Gautier's office and walked over to the elevator to press the down button. Thoughts blazed through his mind, creating his to-do list. But first thing's first – as soon as he was out of the building, he needed to call Ari. The rest could wait.

As he descended in the elevator, he dialed Ari's number, holding his mobile phone and waiting to clear the ground floor of Interpol. As soon as he was in the clear, he hit send to connect the call; he could hardly contain his excitement.

"Ari, it's David... JACKPOT!"

"David, thank heavens. What did you find out?"

"I told you Jade sent me over to talk to the Director of Human Trafficking at Interpol. I think she might have ID'd your main suspect. If we can get to him, we might be able to find Renee."

Ari stood on the bridge of the *Sea Wolfe*, making it's way south in the Indian Ocean.

"Bless you, David. Where are you?"

"I am on my way to the airport in Lyon; I need to report back to the President in DC. By the way, how did you get her involved in your operation?"

"That wasn't me; that was the Raven."

Gray smiled. "I knew he couldn't stay under the radar forever."

"You knew he had a direct line to your wife?" Ari asked.

Gray laughed. "He's not the first ... unsavory character ... to have made his way to Jade's doorstep with important information. You know he helped with the operation against his brother. I came home to find him cooking in Jade's kitchen. Nice guy, actually."

"Seriously?"

"What? You're surprised she befriended a guy like that and brought out the best in him?"

"Of course not," Ari said laughing slightly. "I'm surprised he could find anything in her kitchen worth cooking!"

Gray felt his heart fill with Ari's small bit of humor, thinking to himself. *We've got some answers, another lead in case Renee isn't in Zanzibar. Now Ari can breathe and do what he does best.*

"I'll be sure to tell her you were so astonished."

The laughter from Ari ended abruptly. "You wouldn't dare."

It was Gray's turn to laugh. "I swear, even if that woman *weren't* the President of the United States, we'd both still be afraid of her."

Ari nodded solemnly but not without mirth on his end of the line. "So tell me more about the good news?"

"I think we have located the African connection to the trafficking business; a guy called Tippu Tip out of Zanzibar runs it. He's going to meet his lieutenants in South Africa this week."

Ari was silent, and Gray couldn't tell whether it was static or Ari's heavy breathing he heard.

"Ari, you still there?"

Ari's voice had changed, even the hint of light-hearted banter gone. "That name ties in with our intel here. David, I need your help. I have to mount an operation here to check out Gareth's lead on Renee. If she has been taken to Zanzibar, I don't want to fail her again.

But if we're wrong ... We need to follow your lead, as well. Could you see what is going on in South Africa at the meeting? Handle it? I'll ask Stangl to send a team and resources to meet you there."

"Ari, that is one heck of a request, but you know I've got your back. I'll get Jade to authorize a new flight plan; I'm in a USAF C-32 and can't change the Captain's orders."

Gray could hear some background noise and voices talking. After a short delay, Ari returned to the phone.

"David, you're cleared to fly down to Hoedspruit. Stangl has Jade's private cell phone number, and she just authorized it while we were talking."

"Did she now?" Gray said, "Well that simplifies things, I guess."

Ari smiled. "She said to tell you to watch your back since I won't be there to keep you out of trouble."

Gray exploded with laughter. "She did not. More likely she told you to send her love and kisses and you're too chicken to pass on her real message."

Ari chuckled. It felt good to be in action and think maybe they had a better shot at Tippu Tip with the new information. "I confess. I am not man enough to follow through on her request, but this is me to you – watch your six … honey."

Before Gray could come up with a suitable retort, Ari was back to business. "Stangl is sending a team to meet you there. Their ETA is 18 hours. Good luck."

"Take care, brother." Gray bit off any other response. He'd be sure to let Ari know later – when they were all safely home having a beer in Ari's kitchen – that he had just ruined a rendezvous with Jade at Blair House.

If they were all safe at home … Somewhere out there, sweet little Renee was alone and scared. Gray would do anything for Ari or Jade, but in this case, anything he did, he'd be doing for Renee.

***

Ari knew what he had to do. Down in the hold, O'Flynn languished, Ari's proverbial ace up his sleeve. It was time for Ari to have a personal one-on-one with the weasel pawn of the slave trade. On his way out of the bridge, he reached over to the armament locker and pulled out a Taser, sliding it into the back of his waistband next to his favorite knife. He needed to know the layout of the underground slave chambers in Zanzibar, and he knew who was going to give him that information.

As he entered the hold, Ari found O'Flynn lazing on a makeshift bed of ship supplies. The former captain had fallen hard – no longer the arrogant master of a grand vessel, his bedraggled appearance better suited the ugly inner workings of his soul.

He looked up as Ari came in and smirked. "And so you need O'Flynn

…" Ari remained stone-faced. "Well," O'Flynn said as he rose to a seated position and spread his hands before him, "what's in it for Pedro? Eh?"

In an instant, Ari was across the hold and had O'Flynn against the wall and two inches off deck, dangling by his neck. The smarmy eel had barely a moment to flinch. Bringing the smaller man eye level as he struggled to find purchase with his feet, Ari's glare was pure malice.

As O'Flynn's face began to turn red and his struggles to open his airway became more frantic, Ari said, "Let's start with the right to breathe, and we'll go from there."

O'Flynn tried unsuccessfully to nod against Ari's iron grip, and Ari released him to fall with a satisfying thud to the deck. He lay on his back, gasping for breath for a few minutes before Ari decided he had waited long enough.

"Get up. I have questions and no time left for foolishness." He dragged O'Flynn back onto his bed by the front of his dirty tank top.

"I told you what you wanted to know about the smuggling," O'Flynn said, his voice raspy.

"I want to know about the caves."

"The caves?"

"Don't play games with me, O'Flynn," Ari said, pulling both the Taser and the knife from their carrying places.

O'Flynn's eyes flew wide at the sight of the knife, having already had more than his share of the Taser. He looked to Ari's face, gauging the anger there and concluding murder was not off the table.

"You mean the tunnels beneath Stone Town, eh?" O'Flynn said quickly, holding his hands before him in a sign of surrender. "Yes, yes. I know them."

"Well, then today is your lucky day, *Captain*," Ari let the last word drip with sarcasm. "You're going to draw me a map of those tunnels – every place where they might be holding the children or any other slaves – and then you're going to lead me in."

"Lead you?!" He exhorted, panic stricken, "Cohen, they'll kill us both. We'll never get past the dock!"

"It's up to you, O'Flynn, to make sure we do."

21 THE VOICE IN THE DARK

Renee sat frozen in fright as the voice drew closer. "Just close your mouth, girl. Be good. They don't like girls who aren't good." The voice was harsh, deep and gravelly, the most scary sound Renee had ever heard.

She wanted to run, but felt herself scooting backward against the rough rock floor. Slowly, a face came out of the pitch-black and into the dim light from the torch-lit tunnel beyond their cell door. The face belonged to a girl – older than Renee – with dark skin and hair. But as she drew close enough for Renee to see, the reason for the roughness of her voice became clear – a wound slashed across her neck almost from ear to ear. And her face, Renee could not hold back the look of revulsion that crept into her eyes.

"Go on, girl. Look. See it for what it is – this is what they do to bad girls," the girl hissed, grabbing Renee's arm and pulling her back when she tried to turn away. Her face was deformed – an emptiness behind her sealed eyelid that said she had lost an eye, a jagged gash across her cheek.

"Let go!" Renee cried, wrenching her arm free and scrabbling backward in terror not of the girl's appearance so much as the warning it held for her. "Why …? Why…?"

She buried her face in her hands and sobbed. "Mama, please. Where are you?"

"No one will come for you here, child." The teen receded back into the darker shadows of the cell. "No one good anyway…"

22 Whispered Prayers

O'Flynn had been permitted to clean himself up, and now affected his sense of arrogance if only to provide himself with enough confidence to go through with the plan.

"I tell you we'll never pull it off," he had whined repeatedly as Ari looked over the rough maps and grilled him about dimensions, entrances and guards.

"You have no choice, O'Flynn, so I suggest you figure out a way to make it happen."

And so he had convinced himself that with the major bosses in Tippu Tip's regime meeting at Vuyani Safari Lodge, the rank and file left behind would be easier to con. Back in his white-on-white captain's uniform and fortunate enough that no one outside the confines of the *Sea Wolfe* knew the particular "arrangements" he was under, the plan was simple. O'Flynn would bring in Cohen and the Raven to hand select some merchandise – claiming the Raven demanded to see the operation before he increased his involvement.

He counted on threatening these mid-level men with the penalty for turning away such a profitable deal in Tippu Tip's absence.

As he looked in the mirror for the last time, he corrected the angle of his cap. Refocusing, he saw Ari standing behind him and turned. "My Papa always said no man should live forever."

Glaring, Ari replied, "With the blood in your ledger, I wager you've lived longer than you deserve."

O'Flynn flinched. "Now you sound like my mother."

***

On deck, Ari and O'Flynn found Stangl briefing his teams. One team was already boarding a helicopter to catch a flight bound for Vuyani Safari Lodge with orders to remain just outside the perimeter and await Gray's call if they were needed during his reconnaissance.

A second team, hand-picked by Monique and fiercely loyal to her, would make a landing just down shore from Stone Town and creep in close enough to serve as an extraction team if needed.

Stangl would go into Stone Town with Ari and O'Flynn to "inspect the merchandise." Ari and Stangl were both armed only with a sleek specialized knife completely concealed within the small of their backs.

As the remaining teams broke to gather equipment, Stangl nodded at Ari. "A moment with Tanner and we'll be ready to go."

Ari nodded his ascent and headed for the landing craft … and Monique.

Tanner would remain with his prized *Sea Wolfe* with the hearty, well-trained soldiers and ample ammunitions bunker to protect the children already on board. As Stangl entered the bridge, he clapped his captain on the back. "Are we ready, Captain Tanner?"

"Aye, sir," Tanner said, his eyes on the movements happening on the deck below him. "And you, Pieter?" he asked, his tone softening.

"Fit as a fiddle, Rick. I've got good men – and Monique. It's all well in hand."

"Of course." Tanner could not meet Stangl's eye.

"I know that you loved him as well as I did, Rick. Tonight, we strike our first blow for all the children – in Theo's name."

Rick nodded, seeing in his mind's eye the tiny body wrapped in linen slide slowly overboard and into the sea. "For Theo."

As Stangl turned to leave the bridge, Rick grabbed his arm. "Just be sure you remember you have another son, Pieter. Go for Theo, but come back for Lannie."

It was Stangl's turn to nod silently.

Instead of turning back toward the waiting launch team, he headed below to the play area he knew would be full of giddy children.

Stangl grew more nervous every day that they delayed meeting a second ship meant to transport the children to stay with Jade's parents in Vietnam. They would wait there until the adoption agency (a credible agency with warm hearts that helped them open the back door to Stangl's children) was ready for them.

It kept him connected to his beloved wife, doing good work in her name and helping her parents by keeping them well supplied to care for the children they grew to love. Her father even retired his sampan and spent his days treating every child with the love and care he would have given his own grandson.

With his little farm on the water, no one ever saw the landing craft ferry children in and out, and no one thought twice about the old sampan captain who had disappeared from the city's waterfront. One or two at a time, the children would be resettled through the agency – with full identification that no one ever questioned. *It may be illegal work*, he thought, *but my guys sure are good at it.*

Lannie had based his major on education and was doubling his workload to graduate early. He knew his adopted grandparents were aging and wanted not only to take over the little farm full of children, but to bring them the education he received only because Stangl rescued him from abject poverty on the streets of Ho Chi Minh City.

Some of them – those who had been most abused within the trafficking system – would not be adopted, he knew. But with his help, his father would see to it that they made their way to the states and into respected universities with a chance at a good life.

Stangl stood just outside the play area, watching the children through a small window in the door and listening to the laughter and playful screaming that accompanied the pandemonium within. When he noticed Marie, his breath caught. Off by herself in a corner, the little green-eyed beauty sat bathed in moonlight streaming through the nearest port, her hands folded before her in the purest symbol of prayer.

He knew he should get back to the teams, back to the mission, but he was drawn inside to that little girl. As he walked up slowly, trying not to disturb her, she quietly turned her big green eyes toward him and smiled.

"I have prayed for you, Mr. Stangl. For you and Monique and Ari. God will be with you."

Tears welled up in Stangl's eyes. "Thank you, Marie."

She cocked her head and asked, "Why are you sad, Mr. Stangl?"

"I'm not, child. Sometimes we cry because we are so full of love."

She threw herself into his arms then. "It is always happy to be loved, Mr. Stangl. You need never to cry for love."

If only that were true, child. He held Marie for a long moment, thinking of his own sweet Theo.

"I must go now. Ari is waiting."

Her face showed doubt for the first time. "You will take care of them, won't you, Mr. Stangl?"

He smiled, and before he had time to ponder his response, it was out of his mouth. "God will take care of them, Marie. But I'll be sure He has plenty of help."

She smiled, and as he turned to walk back to the upper deck, he marveled that the words had come out of him at all – a man who found his comfort in an old painting, not an invisible God – and yet …

His eyes rotated to the ceiling seemingly of their own accord. "God, I cannot believe that Theo is not with you in some wonderful place, even though I can't imagine that I'll ever find myself deserving of that grace.

But I must believe in you to believe in heaven, and I need heaven to curb my grief. Hold his hand, God, and cover his eyes; he has always been afraid of the dark, and I have a feeling it's about to get very dark around here."

23 LETTING GO

Ari found Monique in the middle of her men giving them a briefing of her own.

"You are here because you are good at what you do. There are children in those caves that depend on us to release them. Do not let me down."

The last sentence held more venom than Ari expected. *Motivational speaker she's not.*

"NO, MA'AM!"

The resounding response startled him. He looked up to see Monique headed his direction.

"That was some pep talk."

"They don't need a rah-rah speech," Monique said simply. "Each of those men was once a hired killer. They are all seeking redemption before they stand in judgement. I am the gateway to redemption."

The matter-of-factness in her tone disturbed Ari. It was as if she felt nothing for the men in her team – men who followed her almost blindly with near religious fervor.

"That's a pretty heavy burden for you to carry ..."

Her bright green eyes suddenly sparked, and for the first time he noticed how like Marie's they were. "You have no idea what burdens I carry. If you fear for my men; don't. They are all quite prepared to die – more prepared than either of us, I suspect."

Before Ari could contemplate his readiness for final judgement,

Stangl appeared on deck and made his way toward them. He had an odd expression on his face – almost peaceful despite the circumstances of the night.

"Are we ready?" he asked, having no idea that the question could have such a deep meaning in the previous conversation between Ari and Monique.

"I guess the night will tell," Ari said, looking at Monique. She smiled, but it was strained.

Stangl looked from one to the other questioningly. "We are being sent forth with a special blessing," he said finally. As they slowly turned their eyes back to him, he smiled. "Marie has put up a plea on our behalf and says we go with God."

Ari smiled. Monique cocked her head. "You don't believe in God, Pieter?"

He kissed her forehead as he headed for the landing craft. "Tonight, Monique, I am open to anything."

24 Into the Caves

Ari's extraction team arrived at the docks, led by a very nervous Pedro O'Flynn. After a brief exchange with the guards, they were let through. Ari had been right about the guards at the dock – fiercely loyal and also at the very bottom of Tippu Tip's violent food chain. They had gladly let the trio move on to a higher authority.

Judging by the visible scars, Ari surmised he was looking at slaves who had been absorbed into the operation and now passed along a lifetime of cruelty to each newly captured innocent. As vicious as they undoubtedly were, it was hard to hate them for the invisible chains they wore.

"So far so good," O'Flynn whispered, breathing a sigh of relief as the trio left the dock with a couple of armed guards headed for the caves. From the look of the man leading them and the man behind them, Ari wasn't so sure. He glared at O'Flynn for silence. This was still the best way to get into the caves, but getting out was going to be a whole different story.

As they finally neared the strange slabbed opening to the caves, the guard in front slowed and waited to be recognized by a guard hidden at the opening. A light shone out on them, and on recognizing the guard, a large man with a big hoop earring stepped out of hiding beside the entrance.

"Mahrook." The guard moved forward to speak quietly with the large man. After a moment, they both turned to look at Ari and his group. Mahrook lumbered over. Ari didn't like the gleam in his eyes. Mahrook had cocked his head to one side, clearly suspicious. His hand hovered very close to a waist where a khan-jar, the famous curved Arab dagger gleamed in the moonlight.

"O'Flynn," he said without acknowledging Ari or Stangl. "What are you doing here? Who are these men?" His voice oozed distrust.

Ari chanced a sideways glance at O'Flynn, worried that the first sign of an adversary would show him a quaking coward about to sign their death warrants. Instead, he found the confident con man showing a side of his character that Ari had not seen before, a form of believable bravado.

"Mahrook, friend, our lord Tippu Tip sent them. This is the Raven," O'Flynn tilted his head toward Stangl, who had also just as suddenly taken on the full persona of the hard-case Cosa Nostra Capofamiglia – the boss.

"Is there a problem?" he said, glaring at the brute before them. Stangl was not a small man, and yet Mahrook outweighed him and bested him in height by at least four inches. That would make a heck of a difference in hand-to-hand combat with the knife he carried.

O'Flynn stepped between them, "Of course not, sir. My apologies; I assure you this is not the way Tippu Tip runs his business." He turned pointedly at Mahrook. "We would never mean to offend you."

Mahrook looked from one to the other, and seeing no sign of wavering confidence, his own wall of assurance began to crumble. He had no direct line to his boss, who was off meeting with Tippu Tip, himself.

Mahrook knew O'Flynn was connected – and dangerous. He was the kind of man who got himself inserted into big deals, and Mahrook was just a pawn. He struggled with the question of which would get him worse punishment – letting through a liar and a cheat that would never be able to get back out or denying an ally of Tippu Tip himself.

He sneered. *They want in, fine. They'll never get out alive if they cross me.* He handed O'Flynn a torch and lit it from his lantern.

"How quaint," O'Flynn said.

"Oil and rags are still cheaper on Zanzibar than batteries and bulbs," Mahrook said, pushing him toward the opening. "Watch your step. It's a nasty fall."

"You're not accompanying us?" As soon as the words left O'Flynn's mouth, he felt Stangl's sharp jab in his gut.

"Are you afraid of the dark, O'Flynn?" Mahrook said with a smirk.

"Of course not, but I have not been here in some time. Have you changed where you hold the girls?"

Mahrook turned back to his rock seat next to the opening. "Nothing changes in Stone Town."

***

As Ari, Stangl and O'Flynn reached the bottom of the stone staircase, they stopped to regroup. O'Flynn had given Ari a good enough description of the place that he could envision in his mind which way to go next.

"Mahrook works with the doctor," O'Flynn said.

"Doctor?" Ari had again grabbed the front of his shirt.

Even O'Flynn felt disgust, obvious by the look on his face. He responded in a quick disgusted chant. "The doctor takes the organs when there's no reason to ship the children for surgery. There's a nasty little make-shift surgical unit down here where they bring the ones who aren't fit for anything else."

O'Flynn felt the grip on his shirt tighten until it nearly strangled him. He didn't flinch. "I never handled that end of things, I swear. I found ways around it. Couldn't stomach the thought of ..."

He straightened. "I may be a lousy son of a whore, but I have lines I won't cross."

Ari wondered at the vagueness of those lines, but he released his hold. O'Flynn's eyes grew dark. "I've only been here a couple of times – inside. My memory ... well, I don't forget details, but I wish I could forget this place."

He turned to lead them further into the caves. "There are more than children here, you know. But some of them ... Some of them are better left behind."

Ari grabbed him again and spun him. "What does that mean?" he demanded, his face inches from O'Flynn's.

"People can be damaged past the point of being people. Some of these children have not seen daylight in 10 years, some of them are.... It's so sad, Ari. There are monsters in the darkest cells, Ari. What will you do with *them?* "O'Flynn pleaded, trying to help Ari see the magnitude of the problem they were facing.

Ari noticed how O'Flynn had used his first name, as if they were truly on the same side now. For the first time, Ari had to think past the cell that held Renee. They wouldn't all be like Marie. Some of them had been so twisted, they became part of the machine that broke them. *What will you do, Ari, when those broken eyes turn on you?*

Spencer Hawke

25 RECON AT THE LODGE

It had already been more than eight hours since Gray last spoke with Ari. They had gone radio silence en route to Stone Town, and Gray was maintaining his silent vigil just outside the lights of the Vuyani Safari Lodge main deck.

One hundred yards in front of him the Lodge swimming pool was bathed in light. Behind that an outside dinner table was being prepared for the Lodge guests. David could hear the happy banter of conversation coming from the guests as they assembled for dinner.

Suddenly something made a wild dash from the bushes beside him. An immature baby brush hog squealed in panic, running for its life as a full grown leopard ran past David in hot pursuit.

David was too surprised to do anything other than watch, and pray that there wasn't some other bigger predator with him in his sights. He returned to his lonely vigil. *Nice digs,* he thought as he scanned the perimeter with is high-powered night-vision scope.

His attention was keenly focused on the target, but his senses were split between what he saw and the myriad of sounds going off in the trees around him. *Parachute jumps, hand-to-hand combat, sniper school – you name it, I've had the special ops training – but nowhere in there did Uncle Sam prepare me for lions.*

Gray had been well briefed on the area by a local Athena asset, who helped him camouflage his scent. They had found an old campfire, collected all the charcoal, smashed it to a pulp, added water, and then smothered David all over with residue. If only his wife, the President of the United States could see him now, he thought to himself with a nervous chuckle.

The local Athena asset was a game guide, so had snuck David in this far, avoiding the Lodge security teams and secured him in his watcher's post before heading back to rendezvous with Stangl's team.

Gray took a whiff of himself. *I hope this stuff works, because I can sure smell me.* He was not interested in having his story end inside the belly of a big cat.

Within the crystal clear perspective of his scope, he watched the movement of Tippu Tip and his lieutenants. So he has arrived thought David to himself.

Behind the guests, stood an entourage of five Zulu warriors, Askari in one hand, shields in the other protecting them from the evils of the night. Each warrior wore traditional arm and leg bands, making the scene almost surreal. Gray felt almost envious.

So far, all Gray had seen was a veritable food orgy – nothing but course after course of exotic meats and wines as the men laughed and cajoled over whatever they deemed funny in their black business. They had broken their repast only when Tippu Tip saw fit to stumble off for a long nap within the mosquito netting of his posh suite. No children; no women; no slaves of any kind as far as Gray could tell, and no one seemed to be in much of a hurry to get back to business.

26 BENEATH THE WHIPPING POST

The first few cells they came upon were empty, and the hospital suite was quiet. Ari was beginning to think O'Flynn had orchestrated some grand scheme to sucker them into a trap. He turned to grab O'Flynn within the blood stained cavern cell where the doctor had done his dark work. Just then, he heard voices coming their way.

"With Tippu Tip gone, things have ground to a halt, but at least we've had time to dispose of all the … waste." The voice grated on Ari's nerves, a nasally pitch that perfectly matched the slender hands and ferret face that walked into the room.

On seeing Ari and his team, the ferret face abruptly acted as if he had seen something that nauseated him, "Who are you? What are you doing here?" the man said, garbling his words together.

Turning to his nurse. "Get Mahrook." He squealed in a higher pitch,

"Mahrook sent us." It was Ari's cold voice that stopped them both in their tracks.

"You're a liar. Why would Mahrook send you down here?"

"Because he has no concern for you, *doctor.*"

O'Flynn stepped in between them. "We are here on orders from Tippu Tip. The Raven has come to see the girls."

"They aren't here." The doctor never took his eyes off Ari.

"I must have made a wrong turn, doctor. My apologies."

The doctor pried his eyes away from Ari's face to look at O'Flynn. "You. I know you."

"Of course, doctor. I work for Tippu Tip, bringing merchandise for him. The Raven is here to see the girls."

The doctor raised his eyes to Stangl then, who tried his best not to look disgusted. "Of course. There are but a few. The others have already been … dispatched. They are down the tunnel farther and to your left."

O'Flynn made to leave, hoping Ari and Stangl would follow. "Thank you, doctor. We will make our way that direction."

As Stangl finally turned to follow O'Flynn, he heard the man in the bloody lab coat call after him. "Were you pleased with your last order, sir?"

Ari saw it then, not so much a switch but a snap from one personality to another. Where Stangl had stood pretending to be the Raven, there now stood the Raven in all his dark glory. Slowly, he turned back to the object of his disgust, a look on his face as if he had literally eaten something distasteful and was about to spit it out.

Instead, the words poured out like venom just a moment before the knife blade fell. "Actually, I was not, *doctor.*"

Ari sprang from behind the Doctor to clasp his hand over the nurse's mouth before she had a chance to scream, but she didn't so much as move or make any effort to stop the Raven from killing the Doctor. Confused, he released her and looked into her face. Only then could he see the faint scar above her right eye.

"Is he dead?" Her voice was cold, asking for a statement of fact.

Stangl stood up from wiping his bloody knife on the doctor's coat. "Very."

She looked from the body to Ari. "Are you here to free them?"

Ari nodded. He had not fully released her and stood ready to muffle her again if she tried to raise an alarm. Instead, she pulled away from him and began to lead them down the tunnel.

"This way. They will not all go with you. Take the ones you can save. I will take the others."

Ari grabbed her arm and turned her toward him. "What do you mean?"

She smiled then. "I owe them a life of protection and service, Mr...?"

"Ari," he said, with some hesitation. "Just Ari."

"Ari. I have helped them where I could, but done more harm sometimes than I intended. Some of them will not go with you; they can't. But I have ... friends ... on the outside. They will help me with them, shelter them, comfort them. All you have to do is take the ones who can leave with you ..." Her face turned rock hard then, "...and kill everyone who stands in your way."

It was Stangl who answered. "Done."

***

Renee heard the sound first – heavy footsteps in the tunnel leading to their cell door. It didn't sound right, not the slow, pounding steps of Mahrook, and more than one person moving in a hurry.

She hadn't made a sound since the encounter with her cellmate, and hadn't seen the scarred face since it retreated into the deep shadows of the cell. Now, she heard a soft moaning in that direction, and the heavy breathing of panic.

Renee was terrified. Anything that frightened this inhuman girl ...

She heard a key turn in the lock and buried her face in the knees pulled tightly up against her chest. Quietly, she prayed, as the moaning in the darkness took on a fevered pitch.

Hot tears streamed down her face as her imagination fought against her rational mind with images of monsters charging through the door. But the hand she felt touching her own was soft and gentle, and the voice was calm and ... familiar.

"Are you alright? We've come to take you out of here." Renee thought she was dreaming, she had prayed that her Uncle would come for her. But in the deepest recesses of her mind she knew it would be impossible to find her. Yet her subconscious mind wouldn't let her give up, to recognize the futility of her situation. She heard his voice and thought that she was literally going out of her mind, dreaming with her eyes open.

Slowly she raised her head, turning soft brown eyes to her rescuer. "Uncle Ari?"

Ari grabbed the child in a fierce hug. "Renee! Finally!"

"I knew you would come. I prayed so hard. I knew Mama would send you."

"Of course, Renee. Are you all right?" He pulled her back to look at her bedraggled state, clothes torn and hanging from her gaunt frame. He knew the answer, but he had to believe she would be all right ... someday.

Before Renee could find a reply, the moaning in the darkness turned to a blood-curdling scream and the growling of a trapped wild animal. Ari pushed his niece behind him to protect her, pulling his knife out in front of them.

The nurse stepped around him and into the dark. "Bonsoir, Celeste. Mais non, mon cher, ne pas avoir peur. Venez avec Michelle. Come, my sweet one, don't be afraid. Come with Michelle."

It was a long time before the two emerged, the teen's twisted body cradled against the nurse, her head buried in Michelle's embrace.

"She has been here longer than any of us. She knows nothing else. The doctor said when she first came that she was full of fire, and Tippu Tip took it upon himself to break her as an example to the others."

Celeste peeked out at Renee, still clinging to Michelle. Renee smiled. "Thank you, Celeste, for keeping me safe."

The wretched face moved into the tiniest of smiles. "Good girls don't have to live in the dark."

Michelle, the nurse looked over at Ari as she cuddled Celeste, "You must be quick, they have taken the other children to the auction in town, I don't know where it is, but you must hurry."

Ari, cuddling his niece, nodded his head. "Thank you Michelle, we will find them."

Michelle stroked the girl's matted hair. "No, Celeste, ma belle, all of the good girls are leaving the dark tonight."

***

Monique paced the edge of their hiding spot glaring intently into the dark. Finally, the radio crackled to life. They weren't sure they would be able to communicate until they reached the entrance, and no one was sure how they were going to get out of the cave at that point.

"Monique, it's Ari."

"Copy. Are you in position?"

"Negative. We're still inside. We're making our way slowly with a couple of girls and a handful of victims in pretty bad shape. We will release them to your men. Estimate our arrival topside in 10."

"Copy, Ari."

"Stangl and I will surface first and clear a path, but we may need help. There's no one down here – I mean *no one* – and that makes me nervous."

Me, too, Monique thought. *Where did everyone go?* As soon as they knew about the caves, they had staged a lookout on the water by the dock to monitor traffic. There had been no shipments in or out.

LeFeu didn't know what other slaves might be involved in Tippu Tip's organization – men, women, boys and girls – but Ari said there were children in the cell next to him. They weren't there when Ari went back. *So where are the children?*

She moved her team closer to the cave entrance, just within sight of Mahrook, who had no idea that the enemy was watching him. His hulking form sat still next to the cave entrance, all appearances suggesting no one was wise to the operation underway.

LeFeu focused her night-vision scope on the cave entrance in time to see Ari slip out and into the shadow away from Mahrook. O'Flynn marched out as if he owned the place.

"Where are the others?" Mahrook said, standing to look behind O'Flynn into the darkness between the slabs covering the mouth of the cave. Stangl stepped out casually, moving with nonchalant grace to within arm's reach of Mahrook.

"Where is the other one?" Mahrook demanded suspiciously.

"He'll be along," O'Flynn said unworriedly. "I'm afraid my friend here wasn't very impressed with the merchandise. Tippu Tip will not be pleased."

Mahrook looked at him questioningly. "Tippu Tip sent them into town, to the auction." He moved menacingly toward O'Flynn. "If he sent you here, you would know that."

Stangl reached behind him to the small of his back, a single fluid movement bringing the sharp little knife to Mahrook's throat, just as Ari stepped behind the giant and put his blade between Mahrook's ribs.

O'Flynn didn't bat an eye. "Yes, I suppose if he had sent me, I would know that, Mahrook." He began to inspect his fingernails as if bored with the conversation. "Obviously, Tippu Tip did not send me or my …" Even under these circumstances, he thought using the word *friend* might earn him a fate similar to Mahrook.

"Obviously he did not send us. These gentlemen are keenly interested in the auction, I believe. I suggest you tell them what they want to know."

Mahrook laughed. "I am not afraid of your little Americains."

O'Flynn smiled with such pure evil intent that Mahrook began to rethink his sentiment. "Oh, but you should be." He turned his back on Mahrook, and Ari and Stangl dragged him back into the trees and the darkness away from the girls.

"Madam," O'Flynn said, offering his hand to Michelle and helping her out through the entrance, "perhaps we should get your charges to safety."

Renee was the first through the slabs and back on top. She looked around for her uncle and almost screamed when she saw a tall, dark-haired woman and her heavily armed team of men instead.

LeFeu put her finger to her lips. "Shhh," she said with a wink. "I'm with Ari."

Renee nodded quietly.

"You must be Renee." The girl cocked her head questioningly. "Your uncle described you perfectly."

Renee smiled then, really beginning to believe for the first time that escape was possible. Two other girls came up behind her and crowded in close. "She's with my uncle. They are here to help." Renee assured them.

LeFeu looked up to see a woman in a nurse's uniform standing with O'Flynn and a handful of young teens and young adults – both male and female – all badly scarred and disabled.

O'Flynn made his way to LeFeu. "Michelle and I will take them to the dock. We have radioed for help, and there is refuge waiting. They have no homes to return to."

"You will go with them?" LeFeu studied O'Flynn's face. There was such a deep sadness and regret in his eyes.

"If you will allow it, Major LeFeu, God has sent here to serve my penance. I will spend my life attending to these children for the part I played in hurting them."

She believed him. Maybe he was a consummate con artist, and if so, she would find out, and she would kill him. The thought came to her simply, as if killing a man was no longer a burden of conscience. *What have I become?*

"Do not disappoint me, O'Flynn."

He swept his captain's hat from his head and bowed low. "I am indebted, Madam."

With that, he disappeared into the darkness with his charges and LeFeu turned her mind back to Ari. *Where are they?* There had been no sound from that direction in some time. Her brow furrowed in concern.

27 GOLD HOOPS AND GOLD COINS

Anger and defiance rolled off Mahrook in great crashing waves as he kneeled before Ari and Stangl, his hands bound tightly behind his back. He was glaring in silence at their barrage of questions. The sneer lifting the corner of his mouth made it obvious to the two men that he held no fear of them.

Ari studied the mutilated face of the big man in front of him, wondering how far he was willing to go to get information from Mahrook. Obviously, the man was used to vile mistreatment. But Mahrook was defiant, misunderstanding the reason for Ari's intense visual inspection, thinking it was weakness and concern.

"No, little man, you do not scare Mahrook. You can do nothing to me that Tippu Tip will not do a thousand times over when he finds I have betrayed him."

Ari nodded slowly. "You must have been here a long time."

The statement threw Mahrook, and his heavy glare took on a questioning look for a brief moment. "What do you know of Mahrook?" He spat out angrily.

"Nothing," Ari said, leaning back against the trunk of a tree as Stangl stood vigil over their captive, "but I recognize a dog that has been beaten into submission."

Ari could feel the man straining against invisible bonds as he leaned in Ari's direction, eyeing Stangl. "Mahrook is no dog."

"That may have been true once," Ari said leaning down to stare in Mahrook's dark eyes. "Maybe you even had a mother that loved you, though I doubt it."

Ari saw it then – the roll of thunder behind the eyes as the brows dipped even further down, "Or perhaps you were some stray on the streets when Tippu Tip grabbed you. No matter, he beat the fire of independence out of you, taught you his hatred and filled you with his evil venom and unleashed you on the rest of his victims. You are pathetic."

Ari continued his mental torture of Mahrook. "And in return, you have made more loyal dogs for Tippu Tip … and those you didn't turn, you enjoyed hurting the way you've been hurt."

Ari watched as the story was confirmed in the movement of Mahrook's face. As he grew more confident in his understanding of the big man, he grew more filled with hate. Before him knelt a beast who would maim, murder and defile men, women and children; Ari no longer cared how he got that way.

He lifted the razor-sharp blade in his hand, watching it gleam in the dim lantern light. Slipping the tip into the dangling gold hoop, he swept up quickly, sending it flying and rending what was left of the ear in two. Mahrook barely flinched.

"Let's begin," Ari said. "When I have cut away enough flesh to reveal what little soul you have left, let me know …"

***

It had been many minutes since Ari and Stangl slipped off into the night with the Mahrook. LeFeu grew more anxious by the moment, first that something had happened to the two most important men in her life and second that she and her team were sitting ducks waiting by the cave entrance with their charges.

When she heard another muffled scream, she stared into the pitch blackness that covered their trail, desperate to see the two emerge.

O'Flynn and the nurse had left with the worst of them. LeFeu now waited with only a handful of young, terrified girls, and she was impressed at how Renee had stepped into the role of comforter the moment she had seen her uncle. With absolute confidence, she now assured them they were all going to be safe.

LeFeu considered breaking up her team – sending a few men in after Ari – but she wasn't sure where they had gone and knew if Ari and Stangl had failed, she would need every man in her team to even stand half a chance at getting off the island.

"Major, we're sitting ducks here, and dawn will be breaking soon." LeFeu knew she was running out of options. If they were going to rescue the children they had, they needed to move fast.

With LeFeu turned to deal with her team, it was Renee who first spotted Ari emerging from the darkness. She rushed to throw herself into his embrace, but stopped short when she saw the blood staining his hands and splattered across his clothing. Her small face crumpled into a worried brow.

"Are you hurt, Uncle Ari?"

Ari squatted to be eye-level with his niece, "No, Renee. It is not my blood." There was no point in lying to the child about the situation when he knew things were about to get worse.

Renee cocked her head and looked deep into his eyes. "Did you kill him?" Her question held so little emotion that it both surprised and saddened Ari.

"Yes, my sweet."

Renee hesitated a moment, looking down at the blood on his hands as they held her own. "Good," she said finally, looking up into his eyes.

"Can we go home now?"

"Soon, Renee. There are more children in town. I need to help them too."

She nodded slowly. "Yes. We can't leave anyone behind."

***

"… so we don't have much time," Stangl was saying as Ari joined the group, subtly placing his hand at the small of Monique's back for the briefest of moments. She turned to him, and he answered the question in her eyes with a nod. Yes, he was fine, Renee was fine, or at least they both would be.

Mahrook had given them very little to go on, but as his mind faltered with pain, he had divulged key elements of Tippu Tip's remaining security through his angry claims that they would never leave Stone Town alive.

"We know that there are at least a dozen guards with the victims in town waiting for the auction at dawn," Stangl continued. "The victims will be kept out of sight but nearby, since they won't be flaunting their slave auction for the tourists. What we have discovered over the months of investigation is that these auctions are held quite covertly.

"The original Tippu Tip kept a house in Stone Town – a museum now – and in that tradition, the current regime is based in a fortress on the other side of Stone Town. The children will be held in a viewing room there, and Tippu Tip's guests will get the chance to walk through before being treated to breakfast. Then the auction begins. Negotiations are quite civilized and can go on for hours if there is competing interest in any one victim."

LeFeu's eyes danced with fury. "How many guards with the children?"

"That we do not know. O'Flynn's best estimate before landing was five," Ari said. "And we have no idea how many children there are … or even if they are all children."

LeFeu nodded. "We are prepared for anything," she said simply. "We can send these children back with the two team members in the landing craft. I have radioed to have them clear the dock and push inward to retrieve the girls. ETA is five minutes. They will ferry the girls back to the *Sea Wolfe* and come back to await our arrival."

"Excellent," Stangl said. "The landing craft should hold twice our number once the children are safe."

Ari nodded, looking to the rising paleness of the sky; dawn was upon them. "Have your men prepare and help the girls get ready, and we will head to Stone Town as soon as the children are gone."

With that, he turned back toward Renee. As he approached her tight group of children, she glanced up with a smile. *So trusting. Please, Lord, help me be worthy of that trust.*

He inclined his head to indicate she should come away from the girls so he could speak with her.

"Are we ready to leave, Uncle Ari?"

"Soon, my pet. How are they holding up?"

Renee looked back at the huddle. "We are all scared but hopeful."

He pulled her into his arms. "I know this is frightening and I am so proud of how you are caring for the others. There are two men from Monique's team who are coming to take you back to a boat. They will ferry you out to a big yacht where you will be safe while you wait for me."

"You're going for the others?" Her voice shook, but only a little as she raised her chin trying to be brave.

He kissed her forehead. "Yes, love. We are going for the others."

She pulled back then and looked him in the eye. "Will you kill them, Uncle Ari, all of the bad men?"

She deserved his honesty. "I do not know how the fight will go, Renee. If they stand in my way, I will do what I have to do."

She nodded then, and he thought she was satisfied with his justification.

"Then I hope they all get in your way."

28 STONE TOWN

By the time the children were gone and Ari and the team had made the trek around Stone Town to Tippu Tip's modern fortress outside the city limits, dawn had come and gone and the early morning light offered no hiding place.

The team was outfitted in the loose kanzu traditional robes of Zanzibar Muslims borrowed from a merchant's shop along the way. They concealed knives at their waists, but had left the guns and ammo back at the cave as a fallback since they had no way to conceal them. Monique wore a soft-colored cotton kurta tunic.

It was a market day. Stalls of fresh fruit, vegetables and fish were loaded for the shoppers to peruse in the early morning cool. The Raven Ari and Monique blended in with the mob of shoppers in the market down from Tippu Tip's home, watching as men of all cultures arrived and were admitted to the auction.

Ari counted three guards at the exterior that he could see. A recon team returned with an additional three guards at the back and five visible through windows into the interior. They knew the layout of the coral stone, two-story building from drawings O'Flynn had made before coming to the island.

Whatever else that rogue may be, he has one heck of a memory, Ari conceded. He had been surprised that Monique let O'Flynn leave, but not disappointed to learn the man had found a soul inside his seedy exterior.

Stangl, Ari and Monique stood watching the front of Tippu Tip's fortress from within the shade of a merchant's tent. The team had dispersed around the exterior, keeping radio silence until Monique gave them the go.

"This is going to be interesting," Stangl said casually. "How many buyers, Monique?"

"I counted twenty men entering, and my team confirmed that number plus five guards and three men running this *event*." Anger lit the last word.

"We know they keep the victims on the first floor at the back, accessible to the auction floor," Stangl said. "No windows; no way of knowing what we'll be walking into."

"I have briefed my team to take out the guards and contain the buyers," LeFeu said. "They will not let us down."

Stangl smiled at her, touching her shoulder lightly to encourage her to relax the muscles there. "Of that I have no doubt." He turned to Ari. "And the three of us, my friend?"

Ari smiled at the word … *Friend of the Raven, what a strange world.* "We take on whatever is behind the doors with those hostages."

Stangl nodded. "It's elegant in its simplicity," he said of the plan. "Shall we?"

He indicated with a sweep of his arm that LeFeu should lead the way. "Ladies first," he said with a smile.

LeFeu grinned. "I have not been called a lady in a long time, Pieter."

***

The entrance to Tippu Tip's Mansion was a colorful extravaganza of the history of Zanzibar and the early days of East Africa.

Local artists had painted individual tiles, each making up a small section of a grand mural, in all bright colors with significant scenes from the past.

Herds of Elephants marching across the plains of East Africa. A pride of lions feasting over a Cape buffalo, a leopard chasing a twisting and turning Thompson's Gazelle. At the very bottom of the mural, a strange scene acknowledging the early days of African slavery. A caravan of shackled Africans, three abreast, the column so long it continued to the end of the mural. Each row connected to the row in front and behind by a chain that dragged along the ground. The captor's faces too blurred to identify. The only identifiable part of the image, curved scimitar like swords anchored in the belts of the captors.

As Ari, Stangl and Monique approached, Stangl handed an ornately engraved card to a suspicious doorman while Ari and LeFeu did their best to look like they belonged with the crowd of vermin waiting to purchase innocent human beings.

The man looked from one to the other and back to Stangl. "You are late." He said with a slight lisp, as if a part of his tongue had been sliced off.

"Yes, quite. So if you would be so kind as to move out of the way, we'd like to get inside before the bidding starts." Stangl affected his best indignant tone while the man eyed him. Finally, he stepped aside.

Stangl again indicated for LeFeu to enter and Ari put his hand to the small of her back to guide her into the room. She was relieved to find she was not the only woman, and so drew no more attention than she was used to with her beautiful face.

Breakfast was long past, and the bidders were now mingling in a smaller room awaiting the start of the auction. Tension was high, as if each bidder was summing up the other bidders, trying to learn who was bidding for what type of "merchandise".

Stangl saw a face he recognized from Tanner's investigative photos – an upper-level middle-man who was most likely in charge of the day's program. He headed in that direction with Ari and Monique in tow.

"Good morning," he said, again presenting the ornate card. "We arrived a bit late. We had a bit of trouble getting here. We were not present during the viewing, can you grant us access now?"

The man's face darkened. He took the card and looked it over. Recognizing the Raven's symbol on one side and the signature of Tippu Tip's lieutenant on the back, he reluctantly nodded his ascent and spoke in a low voice to the man next to him.

The man inclined his head to indicate the trio should follow him and led them out of the room and down a short corridor. As they went, Monique reached casually behind her to key her mic through the gauzy tunic – three short bursts to let her team know the time was close.

The man leading them was short and stocky. He was clean and well attired. They arrived at a heavy, reinforced wooden door, and he keyed in a sequence of numbers on the keypad.

As soon as he opened it, Ari could hear the sobbing of frightened children. Satisfied that they had gotten past all the security measures that required their escort, Ari reached up to grab the unsuspecting guard, throwing his arm across the man's throat and squeezing so suddenly and intently the guard could not cry out. He struggled against the sudden deprivation of oxygen, but quickly succumbed and Ari let him slide to the floor unconscious.

He looked back at Monique and Stangl before moving forward. The look in Monique's eyes worried him – it was as if she were disappointed Ari had not simply killed the man.

They moved quickly into the room, pulling the door almost closed behind them to muffle any sound of alarm from within.

A guard just within the door looked past them searching for his cohort. Obviously waiting for the guard outside the door to lead these strangers in.

"Who are you? Who let you in here?" His eyes scanned the intruders, looking from one to the other in uncertainty.

Stangl stepped closer to the man, who began to back up but found himself stopped from behind by Ari. Stangl's hand reached to the guard's neck.

"I'm afraid we didn't catch his name," Stangl said, now so close to the guard that the edge of his knife now glinting against the dark skin of the man's neck. "We have come for the children," he said in a low growl.

"You would serve yourself well to let us have them."

The man's eyes were ice, his face as scarred as any other they had come across since landing in the midst of Tippu Tip's men. Stangl quickly gauged that there would be no cooperation, and no easy fight. He heard another guard call out from across the room.

"Ce qui donne? (What's up?) Who are those people, Alain?"

Alain made to answer the second guard, but Stangl whipped him around, and held the guard close in front of him like a shield. "We are friends of Alain, and he was just going to let us leave with the children."

Alain could not respond, the arm at his throat too tight to allow sound to leave his vocal chords. Stangl gave him just enough space to take in tiny breaths. He knew the man would soon pass out and the dead weight would become more of a problem than a solution to the current situation.

"One shout from you, *friend*, and I slice Alain's throat ear-to-ear," Stangl said as the second guard moved toward them. Stangl had seen a glimmer of pain and worry pass across his face. *So they can still care for one another, even if they don't care for these children.* He surmised.

Ari stepped out from behind Stangl, "I think we would all feel much better if you put that nasty gun down, and you might just save your friend's life."

The man looked tortured, glancing from his weapon to Stangl and his friend to the slightly ajar doorway. Ari noted that his face still bore a blazing red scar from his ear to the edge of his lip – surely the line of a knife blade dragged slowly and deeply across his face. Beyond that, he seemed untouched.

"Release the children," Ari said. "We will take you with us."

Monique's eyes flew to his face, an obvious question of his sanity, but his heart knew. *I can save him.*

The man looked to Ari now, and it was there, behind the fear, a glimmer of hope.

Alain was still immobilized, held firm by Stangl, but still he struggled to tell the man, his friend, not to listen, but Ari realized he wasn't even a man, just a young boy, old before his time, but Stangl held fast to Alain.

"Alain, the boy pleaded, we could be free," he eyes begged his friend to understand. He looked to the children huddled in the corner. "We can't do this to them. We can't."

His weapon fell to the floor just as Alain slipped into unconsciousness and Stangl let him drop. The children looked warily at their captor, who in turn looked at Ari. "Now what?"

***

The young boy's name was Jabari – which Monique informed him means fearless in his native Swahili – Ari, Stangl and LeFeu, along with five more girls, slipped down into the tunnels beneath Tippu Tip's home.

Before leaving, Ari and Monique had dragged the unconscious guard from outside in through the heavy wooden door into the children's former holding room, hog tied him and Alain and left with the boy guard.

Won't they be surprised to find two gagged guards instead of five beautiful girls in their little slave room? Ari thought as they rushed through the darkness toward the next exit.

Monique had left her team in place to handle anyone who tried to come after them once their escape was discovered. As they pulled the last child up through a secret grate in the back of a merchant's building in the market, they allowed themselves a sigh of relief that no battle had been necessary with the children in the middle.

That's when they heard the gunfire. LeFeu grabbed her radio. "Jean Paul, report."

The response was breathless. "They just poured out of the house like a hive of bees, Major. We took out the five at the back before they could get to their vehicles."

LeFeu ran to the front of the building where she could see Tippu Tip's home. She could still hear gunfire as his guards, pinned down in front of the house, were fired upon by her team. She wavered, wanting them all dead – and the bidders, too.

"Team 1, pull back. Join Team 2 and head for the beach. Cover our trail and reassemble at our original landing spot. Protect us, Jean Paul, but do not commit suicide for us."

"Oui, Major," he replied as she watched Team 1 scramble back between buildings. She sent up a silent prayer that she would see all of her team alive, and very soon.

Monique turned to her cohorts, very much in charge, "Let's go," she said, ushering the girls toward the exit.

Ari stood with Jabari. Side by side. He couldn't explain why even to himself, but Ari felt an affinity for his new accomplice, he turned to look at Jabari,

"Come with us. You will have a new life." Stangl was standing on the other side of the boy. He must have felt the same thing as Ari because he nodded in total agreement.

Jabari looked at the girls and then back at the house where the gunfire had died down, it looked like Tippu Tip's guards were regrouping.

"No. I have friends here, many of us have been looking for a chance to escape this evil place. I cannot desert them, I have a duty here," Jabari said.

"I know others who will come to me; we will guard your back. They will not get to you."

Ari understood that Jabari felt an obligation to his friends and probably what he considered the only family he had. Ari admired the man's fierce bravery. "Very well, my friend. Thank you."

"No, sir. Thank you. Whether I live or die, I do it as a free man." He turned and disappeared into the market to rally his friends and Ari gathered the rest of the children to him as he and Stangl joined Monique and her team who were guarding their perimeter.

They made good time going straight through the heart of the city instead of around it. The food market was still very busy. The aromas of spices, mixed with the smell of ripe fruit, freshly caught fish crawling with flies, the stench of the sewer than ran through the market walkways like little trenches was all surreal. They running for their lives, the people they passed shopping for survival.

Less than 20 minutes later they were back at the dock, loading the children into the landing craft. Monique and her team stood on shore guarding their backs. When the last of the children were loaded, Ari could see a visible weight lift from her shoulders.

She carries a burden too heavy for anyone, he thought, realizing how much this all weighed on Monique.

29 LIONS IN THE NIGHT

"Ari!" He had barely stepped onto the main deck of the *Sea Wolfe* before he was all but bowled over by Marie. Ari held her close in a tight embrace as Renee looked on. When they parted, Ari turned to Renee with Marie's hand in his own.

"Renee, this is Marie." The girls eyed each. After a long moment, a spark of jealousy flamed between them and then quickly doused by the mutual affection they held for Ari.

Renee held out her hand. "Hello, Marie."

Marie smiled and grabbed her in a fierce hug instead. "I am so glad that you are safe. Ari has been so worried about you."

Renee seemed to melt in the sudden show of pure emotion. It burned through her defenses in a way nothing else had. Watching her, Ari had to turn his head to clear his tears. *Sweet Marie, how she touches us all.*

Dr. Drakul's gentle cooing reached his ears and he turned to see the man encircled in children, each holding a sandwich. Stangl and Monique followed the good doctor and his charges into the lower decks where they could help the children clean up, get changed and find rest. Ari smiled.

Gone was the killer he had seen in Monique. She carried one young girl, gently stroking her soft, auburn hair, speaking softly into her ear as any mother would.

He was drawn away from the vision by the feel of two small hands grasping each of his own. He looked down to find Renee on one side and Marie on the other. Marie tugged.

"Let's get Renee something to eat and I have a beautiful dress that will fit her perfectly."

Ari smiled. "Of course, my beautiful girls. Lead the way."

***

The children were sleeping, and Stangl, Monique and the team had also gone to get some rest, but Ari could not sleep. After they had settled Renee and the other children in the playroom, Ari had gone up to the bridge to check in with David.

His friend was overjoyed that Renee was safe, but now the question loomed, *What do we do with the men at the Vuyani Safari Lodge?* There was no need to ask Monique or Stangl; their answers would be quite clear. But Ari struggled with a conscience that did not always agree with killing men – even when they deserved it.

Ari strolled out to the deck outside the bridge, the wind fluffing his hair. He was alone. In the distance he could just see the East coast of Africa over the horizon.

"So much beauty, so much cruelty," he thought to himself. "It's not as if you haven't dispatched your share of evil men," he said aloud to the empty sea beyond the port side railing. Ari had even assassinated an assassin without the sanction of Athena or the government, and he felt no remorse over the death of Stangl's brother.

But to plan an attack on foreign soil for the sole purpose of killing a half-dozen Africans, even if they were the lowest form of despicable human life on the planet? Jade would be livid, Athena would be incensed, and Ari wasn't sure what his already overburdened conscience would do with it all.

He felt Monique's light touch across the back of his neck. Ari was so deep in thought he had not heard or sensed her approach. He remained leaning on the rail, luxuriating in her intimate touch.

"You're slipping, Ari," she said with a playful tone. "There was a time

I never would have been able to sneak up on you." When Ari snapped his head around at her comment, she was surprised.

His face softened. "Perhaps you're right," he said, pulling her into an embrace. "Maybe I am getting to old and soft for all this spy nonsense."

She laughed and kissed his neck. "Or maybe I am just that good." He couldn't argue with that logic.

Ari kissed her, feeling a beautiful release in the moment.

When he pulled back only inches from her face and her intense green eyes, he found himself wondering what went on behind them that he would never know. As if sensing the scrutiny, she pulled away.

"Have you decided what to do with Gray's intel?" she asked, staring out across the water.

"What do you think we should do?"

Her laugh was course. "I think we should dive into that nest of vipers and wipe it out while we can."

"I agree," Stangl echoed from behind them. Boy I really must be losing it, I didn't even notice him approach. *How long was he watching us?* Ari wondered.

"My apologies, I just came up to ask for our next coordinates. We can't just drift at sea forever."

"Jade won't be happy with a full-scale assault in the middle of Vuyani Safari Lodge," Ari replied, turning back to the sea.

"It isn't McQueen's operation," Stangl said, stepping up to the railing on the opposite side of Ari. "But I don't suppose Burke will like it much better."

Ari laughed. "Not if he can't explain it to the board."

But Ari, in his heart knew Burke might very well be in the middle of that assault if given the chance. He had seen the heat rising off his boss at the thought of human trafficking, no matter what protocols he was supposed to follow.

"It won't change things," Ari said finally. "Cutting off this head won't kill the snake."

Stangl shrugged. "The snake grows more heads, it's true. So we keep cutting. Eventually, the snake grows so short, he won't be able to strike." He smiled at Ari. "Your heart is a beautiful thing, my friend. I wonder how you have kept it so intact for so long doing what you do."

Ari did not look at him. "So do I."

***

It seemed like the entire crew of the Sea Wolf had been exhausted by the operations that day. By four bells, the only light on board came from the bridge where the night watch maintained their lonely vigil.

But one good night's sleep, and Monique's team was ready to go again. As dawn broke through the eastern horizon, Monique with her team was assembled along with Stangl and Ari ready for the next phase.

Vuyani Safari Lodge was calling.

By mid afternoon their flight had landed at Hoedspruit Airport in the eastern reaches of South Africa's Limpopo Province close to Kruger National Park. From there a helicopter carried them to their base camp, just outside of the thousands of acres maintained exclusively for the Lodge guests. The late afternoon sun was going down as they huddled around a campfire brewing some tea. They were within hiking distance of the lodge, and Ari and Monique sat with the team as the local Athena asset briefed them on the terrain ahead – and all its dangers.

David Gray was maintaining radio silence in his perch overlooking the living area of the Lodge. Ari knew it was time to talk to his friend.

He tapped his comm mic three times, David answered.

"What?"

David heard and recognized Ari's sardonic voice.

"I've come to rescue you again." He told his friend. David did not want to give away his position, so just responded.

"Roger, out."

Their plan called for an attack shortly after midnight, so it was still too early for Ari, Monique and Stangl to lead the incursion team in to meet up with David.

While David was waiting in his nest, Ari and Monique paced around the base camp, waiting for the seconds to slowly pass by. Ari and the team started their preparations, more lion deterrent was prepared. He looked at the Athena asset,

"I sure hope you didn't cook any meat over this charcoal." Ari knew how well the King of the Jungle could sniff out his next meal, he didn't want to unwittingly be on the menu.

After he was covered in charcoal residue, that he was sure would deter a lot more than lions, at least he hoped so, he walked over to Monique, who sat in the middle of her protective team, talking in very hushed tones. Ari just joined them, waiting out the minutes. After a long silence, Monique asked softly, "What will you do after…"

Ari had been wondering that as well. "I'm not sure. Maybe I am too old to go on with Athena – with spying." He had been thinking he would have to leave Athena to stay with Monique.

"You would give up everything to be with me?" Her eyes told him her heart was frozen, waiting for his answer.

"You," he said, squeezing her hand, "*are* everything."

He saw the tears form in her eyes, but she refused to let them fall, turning away quickly so Ari wouldn't see. She nodded and turned back to the task at hand.

***

It was time - The guide led them toward the nest where David perched. The team was soon familiar with the hand signals that were passed down the single file line. The sounds of the Jungle, the whoop whoop of hyenas, the grunts of lions were soon the only sounds heard. After 30 minutes they approached a small river they had to cross. A hand signal was passed down the line, Ari didn't recognize it, a hand closing repeatedly towards a thumb.

Ari tapped the person in front of him, repeating the hand signal then shrugging his shoulders, as if to say.

"What the heck is that?"

He was not very happy with the response he received.

"Crocodiles" Ari gulped, opened his eyes even wider, not sure whether there was more danger in the water or on the banks.

He had never been happier to see his old friend. David Gray marveled at how little he heard of their approach before he turned to find eight men and a beautiful woman standing behind him. Not even questioning if he *should* have heard them, he preferred to know that the team covering his back was *just that good.*

"Ari," he said, as his friend scrambled up to Gray's perch on his belly.

"David." Ari said in return. "I don't think I have ever been so glad to see you." David looked questioningly at Ari, who whispered back.

"I'll tell you later."

They lay in silence a moment as Ari looked over the lodge. Everything below them was silent in the early morning chill. "Any change?"

"Nope. Drunken gluttony. If all corporate retreats were like this one, capitalism would grind to a halt."

Ari nodded. "Gotta plan?"

"Nah. You're the planner. I figure as long as we storm the place while the Zulu aren't in there, your eight men should be more than a match for his drunks." Gray grinned a wide, toothy smile.

"Ahem," he heard from behind him. He looked over his shoulder to see Monique with her hands on her hip, he realized his slip up.

"Sorry, her eight men?"

Ari inclined his head toward Monique,

"Major Monique LeFeu, David Gray."

Gray grinned the toothy smile again. "Pleasure."

"Oof." Ari's elbow connected with his ribs. "What?"

"Try to stay on task, brother."

Gray just grinned. "I am, but I can multi-task too."

Monique rolled her eyes. "I say we go with the half-wit's plan."

Gray looked back at her with mock pain,

"Half-wit? Really? You are SO uninvited to Thanksgiving dinner."

"She chuckled softly and shook her head.

"From what I've heard of your wife's cooking, that is not a bad thing."

It was Gray's turn to jab Ari in the ribs. "Ohhhh, Jade is SO gonna kill you."

"Hey!" Ari scowled. "I only speak truth. Can we focus, people?"

He knew a little levity before the fight was not necessarily a bad thing – a steam valve releasing before the pressure of waiting blew them apart. But now was the time to refocus their energy and attention.

"Back to the business at hand," Gray said, his Navy SEAL persona slipping firmly into place. "There are only two of Tippu Tip's men that are visibly armed at any time that I can see – two big guys with REALLY big knives."

Ari couldn't help himself. "It's not the size of the knife, it's how you use it."

The comment earned him another eye-roll from Monique. "Boys." She whispered in mock exasperation. "What, no guns?"

"They came in with guns – all of them – but other than when they have gone out looking for game, they don't carry the other weapons around the lodge. I think they feel they are safe within the compound."

Listen to David, trying to impress my girl. Hold your own in hand-to-hand combat if you want to earn Monique's respect. He thought.

"Ok then," she said. "When are the Zulu present?"

"They are only gone during the heat of the day," Gray said. "I figure all the beasts are resting, so the Zulu do too."

"So our best bet is to wait until everyone – beasts of the field and the man-beasts in the lodge – takes a nap and then sneak down there and wipe them out?"

"Wipe them out? Are we on hunt-and-kill mode?" His question was for Ari and, looking past him, Stangl who had yet to enter into the discussion.

"I will follow the conscience of your friend, David," Stangl said, "for I fear my own is not so finely tuned."

Gray knew what that meant. Everyone wanted to kill the bad guys except Ari. What he didn't know was where he fell on that scale.

"For the sake of my domestic tranquility, I must advise that we seek to capture and detain…first."

Ari laughed softly, but there was no joy in it. "Yes, your lovely wife would be unhappy with the hunt-and-kill plan." He looked first to Monique and then to Stangl. "We go in locked and loaded, and we take prisoners if we're able."

Stangl nodded affably, but Monique remained stoic. "If we are able," she said with a robot-like lack of emotion.

***

The Zulu warriors had been gone for more than half an hour before the team felt comfortable making their move. Thomas skillfully led them around to the least protected side of the lodge and along the wall, beneath its windows.

The plan was to hit Tippu Tip's room first – capture the snake's head and hope the body surrendered.

Ari and Monique had four men with them crawling along the patio toward Tippu Tip's door. Stangl and Gray came at the patio from the other side with two men and Thomas had the other two at the back of the lodge waiting to reinforce wherever they were needed. These men with Thomas were the most heavily armed, the others having left their heavy weapons with them in favor of stealth.

Monique signaled for her men to stop and wait while she and Ari moved into the room. They could hear the hulking man snore from within his mosquito netting. A smell of liquor and sweat permeated the room. Monique looked at Ari, and the killer was back in her eyes. The metamorphosis Ari witnessed in Monique shocked Ari. He had seen her in combat mode before, but this, this was a Monique that frightened him. To her, this was the man she could blame for all of it, for her sister's condition. He knew then that there would be no holding her back.

Ari tried telling her to hold still with his eyes; he would move on the man in the bed, but she pushed off his shoulder moving forward. He wondered at the fact that he didn't try to stop her – or follow. He waited in case she needed him, but did not move to either stop or be part of what was coming next …

When Tippu Tip's bloodcurdling screams ripped through the jungle heat, Ari sprang into action. Jumping to his feet, he looked to Monique, expecting to find she had slit the man's throat, and was repulsed to find the blood pooling much lower on his body. Ari just hoped she had immobilized Tippu Tip before she started removing his manhood.

His shock and disgust must have been obvious to her, but the hatred on her face never wavered with regret. She plunged her knife into the carotid artery of the man writhing before her and turned back to follow Ari as he raced into the patio to join the fray.

Previously unarmed men now had knives and guns, and had Gray and Stangl trapped. Tippu Tip's guards had come across David and Pieter on the edge of the patio as they raced to help Tippu Tip, but we're not able to get by them. That had bought Monique and Ari the extra time they needed to finish off the monster.

As Ari and Monique emerged, Tippu Tip's men turned at the sound, and chaos broke free.

Thomas and his men rounded the side of the lodge to find the patio a bloody battlefield as men threw themselves at one another. With the surprise entrance of Ari and Monique, Gray and Stangl had been able to close the gap and we're now engaged in hand to hand combat with Tippu Tip's guards.

What remained was close, brutal, vicious combat. Gray was getting up-close and personal with those REALLY big knives he had seen. Two of Tippu Tip's men lay wounded, one dead; and Monique had lost one team member, as well.

Thomas fired his assault rifle into the air, grabbing everyone's attention.

"Anyone who does not know Thomas should get to the ground now," he said with a threatening lilt. "And everyone who does know Thomas should take a step this direction." The result was amazing, the brutal hand to hand combat stopped immediately. The guard that had survived the initial combat with Pieter and David hesitated then charged at Thomas with his knife wielded in front of him. He didn't get six feet. Thomas fired one shot to the head, the guard fell to the ground. The resistance from the rest of Tippu Tip's men evaporated.

Like a choreographed dance, all moved as directed, and as the air cleared and the bodies parted, Ari looked around for Monique.

He was not prepared for what he found. Her pale face was on the ground face up, pinned down by a dead guard. Franticly he pulled the body of her assailant off of her, reeling at the blood covering her and pooling beneath her body. Her breath came slowly and so shallow that he had to strain to hear it.

He leaned down, looking for her wounds, trying to find a way to help. She grabbed his hand, her grip like iron despite her fading strength. His other hand flew to the gash across her throat from which a crimson tide ebbed.

"No, no, no," he whispered in agony. "Monique, no. Stay with me."

She looked into his eyes, and gone was the killer, the woman who maimed evil men, gone was the confident spy he had first met. Here was Monique – no. Here was Katarina, frightened girl, afraid and reaching out for comfort.

He kissed her brow and leaned his face close to hers so he could whisper. "Katarina, my beautiful girl, do not be afraid. Where you are going, there is peace; there is safety; there is rest." He pulled back enough to see her fading green eyes, so like little Marie.

"I don't deserve—"

"Shh." He kissed her lips. Her breath was less than a whisper. "It isn't about what we deserve. It is a gift, remember? Marie told you."

She nodded her head, and the slightest smile played across her mouth. "A gift."

Ari's tears fell into her dark hair as he stroked her head. "Yes, my love. Lay down your burden. Let yourself be forgiven."

"I *am* sorry." She whispered so faintly Ari had difficulty hearing her last three words.

He nodded. "I know, dear one." He felt her hand release his, watched as her eyes lost their light.

30 A FATHER FOR MARIE

Renee held Marie's hand as Ari and Stangl helped bring Monique's body on board. They hadn't taken the time to wipe off the lion repellent, so the black charcoal on their faces was smudged by the tears streaming down their faces.

As soon as Monique was on board, Renee and Marie had pulled one another into a tight embrace. They followed Ari and Pieter, silently sobbing, their small bodies shuddering with emotion as Monique was carried to her stateroom and placed on her bed.

Dr. Drakul stood by solemnly, tears rimming his own eyes. "We will see to her," he told Stangl, nodding to his nurse.

"Yes," Stangl nodded absently, still looking at Monique's face. In death she looked more peaceful than he had ever seen her. "I'll call Elena."

The doctor's tears fell then, and his hand flew to his quivering lips. "Oh, her sister. What it will do to her …"

Stangl clapped him on the back. "Steady, doctor."

Marie and Renee stood behind Ari as he ran his fingers through Monique's hair, silent tears still falling. The girls seemed unsure of what to do, and Ari seemed unaware of their presence.

Stangl held out his hands. "Come, sweet ones. Let's give him a moment."

They moved toward him reluctantly, and he took them to his office, rather than back to the playroom. They were in no mood to be with the other children, who had not yet been told about Monique.

He settled them on his overstuffed couch with a cup of cocoa each and some cookies that neither touched.

"Mr. Stangl," Renee asked as he stood staring at his painting. "When will I go home?"

He turned to smile at Ari's niece. "Your mother is coming to get you. I have sent for her and she will come on board tomorrow morning."

He was rewarded with a bright smile, but when they turned toward Marie, any brief light of joy was gone.

"Ari will not want me now," she said.

Stangl went to the couch and sat beside her, pulling her into his lap and snuggling her against his chest. "Why would you say that, little one?"

"He and Monique were going to be my parents, but now she's gone, and he's too sad."

Stangl knew the truth of her words as much as she did. *Bright girl.* "He is sad, Marie. And he may be sad for a long time."

"Where will I go now, Mr. Stangl, without a Papa?"

He rocked her gently, humming an old nursery song his grandmother had sung to him when he was a boy. "Well, if you want, Marie, you can stay with me."

The words were out before he even thought — but when he did, the answer seemed ... *right.* Marie pulled back enough to look up into Stangl's eyes, gauging the truth of his statement.

"You would be my Papa?"

He smiled. "I would be honored, ma petite."

She seemed to consider the proposal for a moment and then snuggled back against his chest. "Yes, I think that would be very good. Together, we can take care of all the others."

"Others?"

"We can't leave any behind, Mr.—Papa. You and I will have to save them all."

He hugged her tight. "Well, my girl, we will certainly have to try.

31 Author Spencer Hawke

Spencer Hawke was born in England and educated in the United Kingdom. He set off as a young boy seeking adventure abroad, and at the age of 21, he and a friend took off for Africa and crossed the continent North to South through the Sahara, sometimes on foot when their old Land Rover did not want to travel as far as they did.

Eight months later, having dodged many conflicts and machine-gun-toting patrols, the pair rolled into South Africa bound for Australia, determined to swim the coral of the Great Barrier Reef. But fate had a different plan for Spencer. In Johannesburg, he met a Brazilian girl who professed undying love for the young Brit. He changed his ticket and flew off to Rio de Janeiro in search of his love.

Once in Rio, she was nowhere to be found, and short on funds, he was forced to get a job. He went to work for General Motors in Sao Paulo. Eight years and two children later, he again had enough money to take off for what he thought would be his final destination.

Spencer landed in Oklahoma in the middle of the 1980s oil boom, and he and his children made a home for themselves in Oklahoma City.

Today he is raising another gift from God, grandson Devon, who is already as avid adventurer as his grandfather.

Find Spencer on Facebook at www.facebook.com/spencer.j.hawke. Connect with Spencer, learn more about the Ari Cohen Series and enjoy his blog, the Weekly Debriefing, on his website: www.spencerhawke.com   and   www.spencerhawkeauthor.com

Spencer Hawke's other Works

Journey of the Bell, The Ari Cohen Series, The Beginning
http://www.amazon.com/Journey-Bell-Ari-Cohen-Beginning-ebook/dp/B00X18WVL4/ref=sr_1_1?s=books&ie=UTF8&qid=1438881406&sr=1-1&keywords=journey+of+the+bell

The Arrows of Islam, The Ari Cohen Series, Book 1
http://www.amazon.com/Arrows-Islam-Ari-Cohen-Book-ebook/dp/B00MO01QXY/ref=sr_1_1?s=books&ie=UTF8&qid=1438881452&sr=1-1&keywords=The+arrows+of+Islam

The Swiss Conspiracy, The Ari Cohen Series Book 2
http://amzn.to/13P3HhK

Mystery of the Dead Sea Scrolls-Revealed
http://amzn.to/13sprAF

Also available in Portuguese
http://amzn.to/1yWBPpq

And in an English-to-Portuguese Translation
http://amzn.to/1BNK3i0

Spencer Hawke

CPSIA information can be obtained at www.ICGtesting.com
Printed in the USA
LVOW07s0927061215

465612LV00020B/868/P